BEFORE I SLEEP

BY

PHYLLIS OWEN

Published in 2009 by New Generation Publishing

Copyright   Phyllis Owen

First Edition

BEFORE I SLEEP

By

Phyllis Owen

A story for children 12 – 15 years

Emma, fifteen-year-old Springbok gymnast, while practicing a triple roll on
a trampoline, slips and hits her back on the metal frame. She is rushed to hospital and horrified when the doctor tells her that she has broken her back and that her legs will be paralyzed. When the plaster was removed and she was allowed home, her father breaks the news that the following day she would be taken to a home for the disabled. She was horrified. At the home were children with various disabilities. She was surprised to find that they laughed and teased each other. Her sorrow turned to anger and she was shunned because if her nastiness. She and her roommate became good friends. One afternoon they mischievously strayed from the home into the fields and only just avoided tragedy. Emma gradually realizes that there's more to life than gymnastics.

CHAPTER ONE

In the beginning

'Don't touch her!' Mr. Wilson, Emma's coach, shouted urgently as, out of the corner of her eye, she saw another gymnast run to her assistance.

Emma had been practicing a triple roll on the trampoline and had misjudged its length and hit her back heavily on the metal frame.

Mr. Wilson, who was some distance away at the far end of the gymnasium, had been watching and saw that she was launching herself from the wrong position. He shouted a warning, but was too late. She heard running footsteps as, with a cry of pain, she collapsed in a heap on the floor.

'Call an ambulance,' insisted Mr. Wilson.

Emma faded into oblivion. She awoke later in the ambulance wearing a neck brace and stared at the young paramedic sitting beside her.

Immediately the blood rushed to her face and a sense of panic threatened to overwhelm her. 'What happened?' she whispered, fearfully.

'You've hurt your back and must lie still,' he replied, flatly. 'We'll soon be at the hospital.'

Emma caught her breath and stared anxiously at him. This was no time for her to be out of action. She was a Springbok gymnast and within a month she was to take part in an international gymnastic competition in Oslo. Her coach had warned that as from the following week she would have to practice daily.

'I must get back into training,' she gasped. 'It's very important that I do.'

'That'll depend on the doctor,' said the young man, in the same flat tone.

Emma gave him a quick troubled glance and a feeling of impending doom came over her. She moistened her lips and was about to ask him why her legs felt as if they didn't belong to her when the ambulance stopped. The door opened and she was carried into the hospital. Her mother and father came running down the corridor towards her, their faces distraught.

A nightmare feeling came over Emma that things were going to get worse, much worse, and she burst into tears.

'Please don't cry, Emma,' said Mother in a soothing voice and smoothed her hair back.

Mother was short, pretty and inclined to plumpness, normally good-natured, with cropped dark curly hair and large brown eyes. Emma was so much like her in looks, but that's where the similarity ended. Whereas her mother was short, Emma was tall and wiry.

Taking Emma's hand, Mother patted it gently. 'Everything's going to be all right,' she promised.

'You really think so?' Emma demanded.

Mother looked ill at ease and added hastily: 'The doctor will examine you.'

The doctor on duty was waiting for her. 'I'm Doctor Barry,' he said kindly, giving her a broad smile. 'What have we here?' He was in his early forties, short, with thick dark hair, and had a slight limp.

Emma tried to sit up.

'No, no,' Doctor Barry said firmly, 'you must remain flat on your back.'

He examined her and a nurse drew blood for various routine tests. Then she was wheeled away to the X-ray department while Mother and Father sat waiting in the corridor.

The X-rays seemed to last an eternity and went by in a sort of haze. Later, she was wheeled back to Doctor Barry. He was scrutinizing the X-ray plates with a deep frown on his forehead. 'Mmmh,' he mumbled, stroking his chin.

A sense of dread came over Emma and her heart began to thump so fast she thought her chest would explode. Her skin started to crawl as she watched him and then she glanced anxiously at her parents. Their faces were like masks and that sent a chill down her spine.

Something was obviously very seriously wrong and she felt frightened, really frightened wishing with all her heart that she were home, safe and sound and that this day had never happened.

Eventually, Doctor Barry stood up and limped slowly towards her.

She bit her lip and looked tearfully at him.

The next few minutes were to remain indelibly imprinted in her memory.

'My girl,' Doctor Barry said, softly, his dark eyes gentle, 'you've fractured two vertebrae in the lower spine, the lumber region, and the spinal cord has been severely damaged. You'll have to go into plaster.'

Emma gave a gasp of dismay and stared at him incredulously. Go into plaster! How unbelievably gross! 'For how long, Doctor?' she demanded, her heart beating fit to burst.

His eyes narrowed. 'For at least six weeks.'

She stiffened at the words and gaped at him in horror as she began to grasp the full meaning of what he had said. What about her training program for Oslo? She had to be ready in a month, almost to the day.

'But that's impossible!' she gasped.

A long moment of silence followed. Doctor Barry stood there shaking his head slowly. Then it dawned on her that she would have to miss the championships. She couldn't handle it and found herself crying like a small child.

Mother's arms went around her and she heard Doctor Barry say, 'There now, lass. The time will soon pass.'

An angry retort rose to her lips and as she was about to speak, she caught a strange flicker, it could have been pity, that came into his eyes. She stared uncertainly at him and pressed her trembling hands to her lips.

'There's more?' she whispered, tremulously.

A taut silence settled in the room. She glanced at her parents. They were as still as statues.

Doctor Barry slowly nodded and sighed. 'Your legs will be paralyzed only time will tell the degree of paralysis. But don't worry about that now. You just need to concentrate on getting well.'

Emma stared at him in horrified disbelief, too stunned to reply at first and glanced wide-eyed at her father. His face was ashen, so very white that he appeared almost ghostlike. Why should he be so pale, Emma wondered? Then gradually Doctor Barry's words sank in. 'Your legs will be paralyzed,' he had said.

'Paralyzed! Do you mean I may never walk again?'

'Yes, my dear, I mean just that. But stranger things have happened.'

'Oh, no!' she cried, 'No, no noooooo.'

Mother, shivering slightly, gripped Emma's hand. There were tears in her eyes and her lips quivered.

Doctor Barry walked to the door and called, 'Nurse!'

Everything that happened after that seemed unreal as though she was moving through a dream, a bad one. An hour later, encased in plaster from under her arms to the tops of her thighs, she was wheeled into a semi-private ward and lifted onto a bed. The nurses raised the top portion of the bed slightly and placed a pillow under her lower spine. She was relieved to see the other bed in the ward was empty. Sharing the ward with a stranger would have been the pits.

'We'll be in to see you soon, but if you need us,' said one of the nurses, placing a switch in her hand, 'just press this.'

Numbly, Emma nodded and they left.

She lay alone in the bleak, empty ward. Waves of self-pity were overwhelming her. It was all so unfair, she thought, tears streaming unchecked down her face. Why me? I'm a top Springbok gymnast, the best in the country. Why couldn't this have happened to someone else? She suddenly felt tired and cold and nausea stirred in the pit of her stomach. Not once in all her fifteen years had she ever been in a hospital before. Glancing around the ward she made up her mind she didn't like it there and never would.

In a short while Mother and Father joined her. She took one look at their stricken faces and once again dissolved into tears. They tried to console her.

'I'm a cripple,' she choked through the tears. 'A crock!' she almost screamed. 'No good to anyone.'

'You're talking nonsense now, Emma,' put in Father firmly. 'You're alive and that's all that matters for now. Anything else that has to be faced we will do that later. Do as the doctor said, concentrate on getting well.' He tried to smile, but she could see sadness clouding his eyes.

'It would have been better to die,' she retorted, bitterly.

'Don't talk like that,' Mother put in quickly. 'Life is precious, my girl, I'll have you know.'

Emma bit her lip mutinously and turning her head from them, asked, 'What about the competition? It's in a month's time. You'll have to phone Mr. Wilson. He was depending on me.'

'You're not to worry about a thing. We'll tell Mr. Wilson.' Father tried to sound cheerful, but he wasn't succeeding. He patted her hand. She snatched it away and her face darkened. She had been looking forward, so much, to going to Oslo and taking part in the competition. Now she'll never have another chance, ever. It was all too much. She groaned, swallowing back a sob.

'Don't lose heart,' Mother tried to reassure her. 'You have other talents. You'll also find hidden talents you didn't know you had.'

Emma bit her lip hard. 'In other words, I'll never be a gymnast again!' The words came out louder than she had intended them too.

A muscle twitched in Father's cheek and he opened and closed his hands, something she knew he did when he was worried or annoyed. Reaching down, he touched her arm, his hand moist with perspiration. 'As your mother said, you have other talents.'

All Emma could do was stare at him in bewilderment. He was a large and powerfully built man with fair hair receding from the temples and very dark violet blue eyes, that almost seemed black.

Her mouth dropped open and for a moment she was speechless. 'So you also believe I'll never walk again,' she whispered, a lone tear rolling down her cheek. 'Where is all that positive thinking you are always bleating on about.'

Father's face reddened. 'I won't tolerate rudeness, Emma.' He looked at his watch. 'We must get back to Stacey.'

Stacey was Emma's younger sister. Very serious, and at twelve already considered to be a brilliant scholar. Unlike Emma, she had no interest whatsoever in sport. Although Emma enjoyed school and did well in her examinations, sport, particularly gymnastics, was the great love of her life.

Mother said brightly, 'We've ordered a television for your room and we'll visit you this evening.'

'Thanks,' Emma muttered mechanically. For a moment or so she could only stare dumbly in front of her.

It was as if her brief expression of gratitude had come from some remote corner of that cold, spotlessly clean and cheerless hospital ward.

****

CHAPTER TWO

Shattered Dreams

Emma tried at first to hold on to the illusion that Doctor Barry had either been completely mistaken or had exaggerated the effect the damaged vertebrae would have on her legs. She dropped off to sleep each night reassuring herself over and over again that the next day would see her moving her legs, even slightly. Sometimes she wondered if she were dreaming and that she would wake up finding that none of it was true.

But, as each day wore on her legs remained immobile, two limbs that were still a part of her, but were no longer hers. Until a short time ago they had helped to send her twisting and turning gracefully and effortlessly through the air.

'Now look at them,' she moaned, 'they are lifeless and useless, like two pieces of washed up driftwood.'

Only four months ago she had competed twice in Taiwan and returned home bubbling with the news that she had tied for first place with Betty Hue, who had won a gold medal in the Olympic games.

She lay hour after hour staring at her toes. 'I've taken part in ten international competitions,' she murmured, 'and there are my toes, one for each competition. Now they mock me. The thrills and challenges that were once such a vital part of my life have now been taken from me, forever. Is this to be my destiny, to lie around like an unwanted piece of protoplasm?' Grabbing a tissue, she began wiping her eyes viciously. 'Why did this happen to me?' she groaned. 'Life sucks!'

As the days wore on and not even the faintest sign of feeling returned to her legs, the full meaning of the doctor's words stole uninvited into her mind, forcing from her all hope. She could no longer escape from the truth, but neither was she able to come to terms with it, wrapping herself in a shroud of self pity that sent the tears flowing uncontrollably hour upon hour.

Finally, one Saturday afternoon, Father said quietly, 'This crying has to stop for all our sakes or there'll be no more visiting for a while. You'll have to come to terms with what has happened to you.' Though he spoke gently there was an unmistakable note of firmness in his voice.

Emma stared at him wide-eyed, completely taken aback. She was about to open her mouth to protest, but decided against it.

'It's been a shattering experience, not only for you, for all of us, Emma,' continued Father, 'but crying about it won't make it better, only worse. I wish it had never happened, but it did.'

Mother, her eyes also widening, put her hand to her mouth, looking at Emma tentatively.

A flush reddened Emma's cheeks. Father had never spoken so firmly to her before and she knew he meant everything he said. Father never normally said things he didn't mean. A surge of anger flowed through her. How dared he, she thought. I hate him! I hate everyone! It's all very well for Father to talk. He can walk.

Waves of self-pity were overwhelming her and for a while she was lost in her own bitterness. Her mouth dried and it felt as if her vocal cords were glued together. Finally she said in a muffled voice, 'I promise, no more tears.'

Father looked at her questioningly. The tension in the room relaxed and a smile broke over his face. 'Good,' he said, guardedly. 'You've made the right decision for your sake as well as ours.'

Conversation was stilted for the rest of the visit and Emma was relieved when it came to an end.

Something bitter twisted deep inside her and from that day onwards, Emma no longer cried, but showed her feelings of anger and hopelessness in other ways. She came to regard the hospital as a prison from which she wanted to escape, although she had no idea what she would do if she managed to obtain her freedom. Above all, she wanted to escape from her useless body.

She took a twisted pleasure in insulting anyone who talked to her. Because of her rudeness, even the nurses who were good-natured finally shunned her and only spoke to her when it was absolutely necessary. She even surprised herself at how aggressive she had become. 'But I don't care,' she hissed, 'I can't stop myself from hating everyone. It just comes on its own.'

When Mr. Wilson, her coach, came to see her, carrying a bunch of flowers, not even he was allowed to escape her wrath. As he was about to place the flowers in her hand she pushed them away and they fell to the floor. She turned her head away quickly, but not before seeing a look of perplexed astonishment come over his face, as he stood hurt and confused next to the bed.

The matron, who happened to be passing, witnessed her act and stormed up to her. 'Tsk, tsk,' she tutted, 'We've had enough of your bad behavior, young lady. Self-pity won't get you anywhere. You can't turn the clock back, that means you can't change anything so you may as well make the best of it, lump it, as you children would say.'

Emma turned to look at Matron, her face glum, folding her arms in an attitude of couldn't care less, yet she knew she dared not answer matron back as she was a formidable force and not one to be trifled with, easier to argue with a python than matron!

Mr. Wilson hastened to Emma's defence. 'Don't be too hard on her, Matron. This isn't like her at all. I've always known Emma to be polite and friendly and she's well liked by the other gymnasts. This unfortunate accident has been a great shock, but I'm sure she'll soon come to terms with it. She has a great deal of courage and determination.'

Emma said nothing, but avoided looking at him, knowing she had behaved disgracefully and yet not caring.

Then, as if at a loss as to what he should do, he retrieved the flowers and placed them carefully on her locker.

Matron shook her head and gave her that see-right through-you look, and with an expression of disgust etched clearly on her features, walked out of the ward.

Mr. Wilson sat on the edge of the bed and placed his hand on Emma's. She pulled it away. For a moment he was silent. Then he said softly, 'I'm sorry about what's happened to you, Emma. If only the clock could be turned back. I'd give anything for it not to have happened.' He paused for a moment before adding, 'But it has happened and when you are able to forget your disability and concentrate on your abilities, of which I'm sure you have many, only then will you find contentment.'

She turned and scrutinized him. His face showed no emotion, yet his eyes were sad. For a brief moment, there came over her a feeling of pity as he fumbled for words, but the pity left her as quickly as it had come, buried under a storm of anger and resentment. 'That's all I've been hearing from the so-called 'able bodied,' she spat out, her voice rising as she spoke, 'All this sanctimonious preaching, I'm sick of it. I don't want you or anyone else to feel sorry for me.'

Blinking in disbelief, she saw a flash of irritation pass over his face. 'I'm sorry, Emma my girl,' he said quietly. 'I didn't mean to sound patronizing.' His voice trailed off and he glanced at his watch, rising to his feet. 'I must be going now.' Nodding, he walked slowly from the ward.

For some minutes after he had left, she sat with her head in her hands. A momentary pang of guilt came over her. Then clicking her tongue angrily, she snarled, 'Why does everyone always know what's best for me? I'd like to see them in my position.' When the anger left her, in its place was an unbearable emptiness. 'I feel frightened and different,' she moaned. 'Where has the real me gone?'

That was the only time Mr. Wilson ever visited her.

As the days passed she became more and more isolated from the world about her and sank deeper and deeper into an abyss of misery. 'The nursing staff seldom speak to me,' she complained. 'It's as though I'm invisible.'

A thermometer was pushed under her tongue every morning and evening. Food trays were placed in front of her to be removed a half an hour or so later without any words being spoken. She was subjected to what is perhaps the ultimate insult, being completely ignored.

She gave a low stifled groan and tried to console herself by saying that anyone would react exactly as she did if they had to lie on their backs all day and all night for weeks on end.

At last the great day had arrived when the plaster was to be removed. She woke early that morning and looked out of the window. A thunderstorm was building up. Dark clouds lay low on the horizon and there was the far off rumble of thunder. In the sky full of clouds there came the drone of an aeroplane, its sound slowly dying into the distance.

'Mmmh,' she grunted, 'Welcome to sunny South Africa.'

She shivered. The gloom seemed to press against her like a cold, damp hand. She listened to the morning activity in the corridor as the night nurses hastened to and fro attending to the needs of their patients before the day staff arrived.

She waited with a mounting sense of excitement as once again she grasped for the illusion of hope. Could it be that once the plaster was removed she would be able to walk again? She tried to wriggle her toes, willing them to move, but try as she may there was no response.

'It can't be,' she reasoned. 'Surely the plaster must be pressing against a vital nerve around the spine. When someone breaks a leg or an arm, once the bone heals everything goes back to normal. Her friend, Doris, broke her arm and it was stiff for a while so she had to have physiotherapy, but after a few treatments it was back to normal. After all, the spine is also a bone and once that heals surely everything will be all right.' But a hollow feeling of fear gripped her stomach. 'You're just fooling yourself again,' she muttered, bitterly, fighting back the tears. 'The spine will heal, it's the damage done to the spinal cord that's the problem.'

A breakfast tray was placed in front of her.

'Come on, eat up,' broke in the pretty young nurse's aid who had brought it to her. 'Sister won't like it if you don't eat.' She was new in the ward and she smiled encouragingly at Emma.

'I couldn't care less what Sister likes,' Emma snapped, her hackles rising.

For a moment the nurse's aid was taken aback. Then she said softly, 'Ag, shame, you're still hurting about your legs. Foeitog, to everything there's a season. Your sadness will go, Skattie.'

It was Emma's turn to be taken aback. But before she could protest the nurse's aid had left the ward.

An hour later Emma was wheeled into the plaster room, which was next to the X-ray department. A young doctor, with a round podgy face and thick unruly blond hair, whose name was Dr. van Heerden, gave her a warm greeting and smiled reassuringly. A tall thin nurse wearing thick-rimmed spectacles, stood beside him. She gave Emma a wintry smile. Emma nodded a brief acknowledgment and glanced anxiously at Doctor van Heerden.

With a pin he prodded under her feet and along her legs. 'As I thought,' he said quietly, almost to himself. 'No response.'

A whimper of fear escaped from her. 'You mean I won't ever walk again?' she whispered, a sob in her voice.

'Didn't your doctor warn you?' he asked, surprised.

'Yes, but I was hoping…' she couldn't finish.

He bit his lip thoughtfully. 'I can't see into the future. Maybe with the help of calipers later on, who knows, but there's no guarantees.'

The weight of her depression once again pressed down on Emma as she forced back the tears.

'At least you'll be able to have a nice warm bath when we get rid of this cumbersome straight jacket,' Doctor van Heerden said, jovially.

She stared at him wide-eyed and her nerves felt as if they were suddenly on red alert when he took a small electric circular saw, the size of a five rand coin, from the top of a cupboard and walked to her side. She gasped and drew in a long shuddering breath as if it were to be her last.

The doctor gave a deep-throated chuckle. 'Don't worry. You're well padded with cotton wool. I won't hurt you.'

He pressed the switch and a high pitched whine filled the room. She flinched as he began cutting through the plaster. The dust whirled around them. It wasn't long before the plaster fell away and she was free. She breathed a deep sigh of relief. Am I glad that's over, she thought!

'How does that feel?' he asked.

'Good!' she gulped.

With a great effort she managed to keep her voice steady but her lips were quivering. She ran her tongue over her upper lip.

'X-ray time, Nurse. Take her next door. Then she can go back to the ward. Doctor Barry will call to see you later.'

After the X-rays she was returned to the ward to wait for Doctor Barry. When he called he told her she could go home later that morning. For a short while she was elated, then the gloom returned. 'Just remember,' he added, 'Yesterday has gone forever. With determination you can overcome all your obstacles.'

She nodded, groaning inwardly trying hard to hold on to her calm demeanor. Not you too. I'm sick and tired of all the constant advice being bleated out to me from all sides. What gives with this mob? One day I'm going to have a screaming fit and that'll shake them all.

He said goodbye and left.

As she lay on the bed it occurred to her that she would return home a cripple with all her dreams shattered into a thousand pieces. She felt scared. Mr. Wilson had told her that one day in the not too distant future she could win the South African championships and added that, in time to come, when she was too old to take part in gymnastics, she would make a good coach.

These hopes and dreams had always been in the back of her mind, particularly when she was alone in her room looking at the trophies and medals she had won that were displayed in a glass case above her bookcase. Things would be different now, completely different. The glittering trophies and the medals resting snugly in velvet-lined cases would serve only to remind her of the fullness of the past and the emptiness of the future. Instead of pleasant memories, they would be there to haunt her. A deep sadness settled over her.

A nurse came in with a wheelchair. 'Your parents will be calling to fetch you soon,' she announced. 'First you must have a bath, then I'll dress you. You can wait for them on the balcony. I have to get the ward ready for two patients who'll be arriving this afternoon.'

Emma said nothing. The nurse lifted her into the wheelchair and took her to the bathroom. I have to depend on others for even my smallest needs, she thought, clenching her hands. I'm useless, a cripple. My life has been robbed of all its dignity. Once, several months ago, she remembered walking home from the gymnasium with Father when they came upon a drunken man staggering towards them. She felt her father tighten his grip on her arm as the man lurched past.

As Father relaxed his grip she heard him mutter, 'Drunkards seem to lose all their dignity.'

So it was now with her for she was confronted with the ultimate embarrassment of even having to be assisted to go to the bathroom.

During the weeks she had been in plaster the nurses had washed her down in the bed to the extent they were able to, but now at least she could regain a sensation of cleanliness. She lay soaking in the silent heat of the water as the past weeks blurred together like a mixed up mess. She managed to wash her hair and the nurse dried it for her. Later, dressed and ready to leave, the nurse wheeled her on to the balcony and left her alone. There was a metal railing about fifty centimeters high running along the low balcony wall. She wheeled herself to the wall and, leaning forward as far as she could, she and looked down on a car park several stories below. The cars and the people looked like toys.

It was a cold July morning and the air was fresh with the smell of rain. The storm had passed. It had come and gone so quickly early that morning and the sun now shone brightly in a crispy clean blue sky.

A tight feeling came into her chest. There were all sorts of hurts rumbling inside her as she sat watching the people hurrying hither and thither, going places, something she would never be able to do for a wheelchair was to be her constant companion. She could picture children and grownups alike staring at her as if she had two heads, a freak. It broke her heart to see her crippled legs, so frail. All the strength and firmness had left them. Tears began to build up in her eyes, but she forced them back. This wasn't the time to cry.

The sun suddenly clouded over and a strong wind came up. Shivering involuntarily, she glanced at the railings on the balcony wall. A dreadful thought occurred to her. It wouldn't be difficult for me to pull myself over. I've nothing to live for. Things could only get worse. I'd rather be dead than go on for years and years like this, a burden to everyone, a nuisance. Her eyes misted over and the people below became a kaleidoscopic blur.

Reaching out, she closed her hands slowly around the metal railing. It was cold to her touch.

****

CHAPTER THREE

Homecoming

Slowly Emma pulled herself out of the wheelchair and clung to the railing. Her heart was pounding, her hands clammy. The wheelchair slipped backwards as her head swam and her legs folded under her. 'What's happening to me?' she moaned. Try as she may, she couldn't find the strength to lift herself up.

Weak and breathless, she cried out with frustration and anger, 'I've always been able to take the whole weight of my body on my arms. I can't anymore. I'm as weak as a kitten.'

Crestfallen, she closed her eyes and slithered to the ground where she lay helpless, sobbing uncontrollably.

There was a cry of alarm behind her. 'Emma! What are you doing? Oh, my child, what are you trying to do?'

It was Mother. She stood open-mouth in astonishment. Hastening to Emma's side, she cradled her head in her arms. Then, holding her at arm's length, her face ashen, she burst out, her bottom lip trembling ever so slightly, 'Please tell me, Emma, what were you trying to do?'

The tight knot of misery within Emma wouldn't dissolve into words. Instead she buried her face in her hands for a moment before looking up at Mother, her face wet with tears. 'I,' she began and stopped. She couldn't possibly tell Mother what she had intended doing. Yet she felt like screaming it out to one and all that there was nothing for her to live for.

Just then Father stepped on to the balcony and Mother looked appealingly at him.

Without saying a word he gently picked Emma up and settled her back into the wheelchair.

'I tried to stand up,' she lied. Swallowing hard, she brushed away the tears with the back of her hand, and turned her face guiltily from him. He knows, she thought angrily. There's nothing you can hide from him. She had noticed the lines of concern etched deep across his forehead and under his eyes and when that little pulse fluttered in his throat it was a dead give away that he wasn't happy about something and that something was what she had tried to do.

A sudden chill came over her as if the sun had gone behind a cloud. What now, she wondered?

'Let's go home,' Father said, quietly.

She breathed a sigh of relief. 'A reprieve,' she muttered.

It didn't take long to go down in the lift and into the car park. Once outside the hospital Emma felt as though she had just come out of a dream. Everything seemed so weird as though she had been living in another world. She supposed in a way she had been. After Father had settled her into the car, he folded up the wheelchair and put it in the boot. Then climbing into the car he drove away.

After a few pleasantries about how well she looked and how glad they were she was now out of hospital, they drove home. Emma was too preoccupied with her own thoughts to notice their silence.

Her mind drifted back to the balcony and she shuddered. When it came to the crunch, she thought, frowning, would self-preservation have brought me to my senses? Would I really have hurled myself over the railings? Sighing deeply, she knew that at that precise moment, if she had the strength to pull herself over the rail, she would have done it?

Staring at the fluffy white clouds gently rolling across the sky, she whispered, 'It's scary.'

The hospital wasn't all that far from her home, a mere few blocks, and soon they were driving through the gateway. Emma caught her breath at the sight of the garden. There was a profusion of yellow, red and white daisies that bordered the long driveway. She gasped in amazement at the small pine tree they had planted last Christmas. It had grown to almost twice its size or maybe more, since she had last seen it.

'Just look how tall the Christmas tree has grown and how lovely the daises are!' she blurted, involuntarily, then bit her lip and frowned.

Father laughed. 'I'm glad you've noticed. All my hard work has been worthwhile.'

Mother turned and smiled at her. 'It hasn't only been your father's hard work. We've had so much rain the garden's better than it has been for a long time. You're right about the little tree. At first I thought it would never take root. It didn't seem to want to grow, but recently it has just shot up. It's as though it decided that it liked where it was.'

Father stopped the car at the front door and took the wheelchair from the boot. After placing her on the seat he wheeled it through the doorway and into the lounge. Again she felt a strange sensation as she looked around at the familiar comfortable chairs and the bright pictures hanging on the walls. They were the same, but she felt different. Yet, she mused, it was good to be home.

Her joy was short lived when she realized that nothing was ever going to be the same again. Her whole world had been turned upside down. From now on she would be confined to a cumbersome wheelchair. No more chasing down the passage to answer the telephone. She would now have to wheel herself around. How gross! Glancing across at her mother she noticed that she appeared to be restless, as if she was worried about something.

'I'll get us some tea,' Mother said quickly and hurried away to the kitchen.

Emma frowned and faced Father. The set of his mouth and the frown that creased his forehead made her feel uneasy.

As if anticipating what was to come she asked, tentatively, 'How...how...will I be able to go to school?'

Father gave the impression that he had either not heard or was ignoring her question. Then he focused his attention on her, his eyes grave and questioning.

She caught her breath and her hands tightened on the arms of the wheelchair so that her knuckles showed white. Bad news coming, she told herself, I sense it. The silence that followed was deafening.

Finally, 'Emma!' Father began, his face drawn.

'Ye..ye..yes,' she stammered, her lips quivering.

'Doctor Barry and I have had a long discussion about your condition and he strongly recommends that it'll be in your best interest to be admitted, as soon as possible, to the 'Happiness Inn', a school for the handicapped on the outskirts of Johannesburg. There you can continue your education and also, what's even more important at this stage, you will receive the necessary treatment.'

Emma stared at him in horror before exclaiming savagely, 'You want to get rid of me, don't you? You're embarrassed to be saddled with someone in a wheelchair. I'm no longer Emma, the Springbok gymnast!'

Father shook his head and said softly, 'You know you're talking nonsense, Emma, so I'm going to ignore your remarks. We've only your welfare at heart. School here is out of the question and you need daily therapy. Also, the Happiness Inn isn't all that far away. We'll visit you each Sunday afternoon. It's not as though you'll have to live in another town.'

'Big deal!' she hissed, between set teeth. 'That makes me feel a whole heap better!'

'That's enough!' Father's voice was sharp. He leaned forward and stared straight into her eyes. 'You don't want to sit at home all day doing nothing, do you? We don't have the necessary know how to help you and there's still much you can do with your life, but you need help. You may not believe me now, but the time will come when the same cast iron determination that made you a Springbok gymnast will help you to discover a new life that will be just as rewarding. It may never be the same for you again, but it can be enjoyable in a different way.'

Emma looked at him skeptically. 'What kind of new life?' There was an edge to her voice.

Father, with a smothered exclamation of annoyance replied, 'That's for you to find out, my girl!'

Confused and humiliated, her cheeks now fiery red, she spat out, 'When do I leave?'

'Tomorrow.'

'What! Tomorrow! Are you getting rid of me that soon!' she broke in, alarmed, and then added in a chilling voice, 'Take me to my room.'

Father was taken aback for a moment. He sighed helplessly. 'Please isn't a swear word, Emma.' There was a hint of sadness in his voice. 'You'll have to learn to live with your disability and not fight it.'

She sniffed, but remained tight-lipped.

He wheeled her into the bedroom and left.

Once there, she blinked in amazement as her eyes fell on two large bowls of red and yellow roses that stood on her dressing table. Pinned across the pink and white striped curtains was a banner with the words, 'Welcome Home, Emma'. Her heart softened momentarily and her eyes welled up with tears when she recognized Stacey's handwriting on the banner. She angrily brushed away the tears with the back of her hand. 'She shouldn't have bothered. I won't be here long enough to smell them.'

The sunlight shone on the pretty pink and white floral carpet and the air was heavy with the scent of the roses. Her eyes fell on the enlarged photograph above the bed of her receiving Springbok colours and an empty, lonely feeling came once again stealing into the pit of her stomach. She gave a little shiver as if a chill had crept into the room and touched her.

Mother came in carrying a tray of tea. On a plate were two large slices of her favourite chocolate cake. Emma's face stiffened as she regarded Mother for some seconds in cool silence.

Undaunted, Mother told her, 'Father has had to go back to work. We'll have our tea here.'

'You agreed to send me away,' Emma hissed. 'How could you? Some mother you are.'

Mother was taken aback, her eyes sad. 'You need help,' she said. 'There was no choice.'

Emma said very little during tea, only answering her mother's questions in monosyllables. She didn't even discuss her leaving home, which was still foremost in he mind. When tea was finished Mother, after a great deal of difficulty, helped her to go to the bathroom. If it hadn't been for the fact that Mother was able to lean against a cupboard close to the door, they would both have overbalanced and fallen heavily to the floor. It was also because of this cupboard that the door couldn't be opened sufficiently wide enough for the wheelchair to be pushed into the bathroom. Definitely not wheelchair friendly, she thought wryly.

She realized, grudgingly, that Father was right. Mother couldn't look after her. When she placed her once again in the wheelchair Emma said she wanted to rest. Again with great difficulty, Mother lifted her on to the bed and gave her some books and magazines to read.

For a moment she dumbly leafed through the pages. Then she must have fallen asleep for she was awakened by a soft, almost nervous, tapping on the door.

Emma hesitated and then called, 'Yes? Come in.'

The door opened to admit Stacey. She was short with straight blond hair swept back into a ponytail and she had dark blue eyes, slightly lighter than Father's. With a whoop of joy she ran to Emma and hugged her. 'It's wonderful to have you home again, big sister,' she cried, her eyes sparkling with delight. She was glowing with health and vitality.

Emma pushed her away. 'But only until tomorrow,' she retorted. 'I'm not staying as you know.'

She didn't mean her voice to sound so harsh. It just came out that way, but seeing Stacey so full of life and able to walk had upset her. She supposed she must have felt envious. Not supposed, she had to admit. She definitely was envious.

Stacey's face reddened. Shrugging, she stood up. 'It's lunch time,' she said, flatly. 'Mother wants to know if you would like to be wheeled to the table or will you eat here in your room?'

A grim smile came to Emma's lips. 'Wheeled to the table? No thanks, I'll eat here.'

Later in the afternoon Emma lay listlessly on the bed. Mother was busy in the kitchen and Stacey was in her room. Through the open door Emma could hear her moving around and the rustle of paper as she did her homework.

She flung the magazines to the floor and shouted, 'Stacey, come here!'

Stacey came into the room, smiling. 'You called, Emma?'

'Yes I did. Get me the puzzles. Hurry up! Don't just stand there and stare like a mampara!'

The smile faded from Stacey's face. 'Please don't be cross, Emma,' she pleaded, 'Think how fortunate you are to be alive. You could have been killed. Just the thought gives me the shivers.'

'Yeah, yeah, big deal. All very well for you to say that. You can run around while I have to lie in bed or be pushed in a wheelchair. It's easy to smile and be kind when there's nothing wrong with you.' Emma beat her hands on the bed in frustration. 'I even have to be sent away to school. Can you handle that! You all want to get rid of me because I'm a nuisance.'

'Look, Emma, it's not our fault neither is it yours that this dreadful thing has happened, but behaving the way you do only makes things worse. Being angry won't change anything.' Stacey sighed as she handed the puzzles to Emma and sat down on the bed. 'I'll help you with the puzzles if you want me to.'

'Get out! Get out!' Emma screamed shrilly. 'You can walk, run and play games and I can't. I hate you. I hate everyone. I wish I were dead! My whole life is pointless.' She pounded her fists on the bed.

With that she hurled the box of puzzles across the floor. Stacey ran crying from the room.

Emma stared at her retreating figure. 'I can't help it,' she cried. 'I hate everyone, every single person on this earth.' She buried her head in the pillow and was weeping when Mother came in.

'Emma,' Mother called softly to her.

'I don't want to talk to anyone,' she sobbed.

Mother sat on the edge of the bed. 'Stop crying immediately, Emma.' Her voice was low and tight, every word clipped out. 'Whether you want to talk to me or not is immaterial for I'm going to talk to you, and I expect you to listen.'

Emma stopped crying but didn't lift her head from the pillow.

Mother continued, 'We've put up with your tantrums because we've felt sorry for you. You're going through a cruel time. Your injury caused us all a great deal of concern, but you are alive and that's all that matters.'

Mother put her arms around Emma and whispered, 'Feeling sorry for yourself and lashing out at Stacey and hating everyone will make it so much harder for you. This is when you need friends and family. If you continue to behave so badly you'll drive everyone away. Even though we feel sorry for you, you will by your rudeness, become thoroughly disliked. We have to think that a handicap is just another problem with another solution and we are going to help you find it. Emma, do you understand what I'm trying to tell you?'

Emma turned her tear-stained face towards Mother, who hugged her. 'I'm sorry,' she said between sobs, 'I'll try. But it's so hard. I can't help hating everyone. I get so angry and feel so helpless.'

'I know, your wounds, physical and emotional, need time to heal. We'll help you in every way we can. Come now, I want to see a smile.'

'It's a pity I have to leave here,' Emma groaned. 'Is there no other way?'

'No. We have no control over that. It's for your own good. Look upon it as a boarding school,' Mother suggested.

Emma quipped, 'At boarding school you come home for the holidays.'

'Yes. It's a possibility in the future. Once you are self-reliant there'll be nothing to stop you. Happiness Inn has all the facilities you need and I'm sure with your determination you'll overcome your problems.'

'Of which I have many,' Emma murmured to herself, 'starting with going to the toilet, bathing, dressing and whatever.' She clicked her tongue angrily.

That night she lay in bed tossing and turning and going over the events of the day. For once the anger had gone and in its place was an unbearable loneliness as if her spirit had flown out of her. She pulled the blanket up over her chest and lay there for a long time listening to the sounds of the night. Her thoughts kept coming back to the same conclusion. She was a cripple. As she stared into the darkness the weight of her hopeless situation again pressed down on her and she wept bitterly.

****

CHAPTER FOUR

Emma's New Home

They were on their way to Happiness Inn. Father cruised along in the slow lane. All about them cars speeded past. People were on their way to work, Emma supposed. Most cars only had a driver. It seemed such a waste, hundreds of cars with only one person in each one. Her mind went back to earlier that morning when Stacey had come to her room to say goodbye before leaving for school. She had stood tentatively at the door with a concerned, almost bewildered, look on her face.

She had beckoned to Stacey to come in.

'I'd like to wish you well, big sister,' Stacey told her. 'I'm sure once you settle down you'll enjoy it there.' She gave her a quick hug.

'Thanks,' Emma whispered and then burst out, 'Stacey, I feel so weird, like I'm not myself anymore, a stranger. Do you remember the film where a woman had an out of body experience?'

Stacey nodded.

'Well I feel something similar to that, as if I'm in someone else's body. It's so very scary!'

'Oh, Emma,' gasped Stacey. 'I know what you mean. I too felt strange when you were in hospital. Mother and I discussed it the other evening. Our lives are different without you even the house is spooky. We've all had to adjust to the changed circumstances. We miss you so much.'

Emma stared at her in shocked surprise. Then she smiled wryly. 'I never gave it a second thought that all of your lives had changed because of me, but I can understand it now. In a way it's comforting to know how it affected you because I was convinced I'd gone bonkers.'

Their conversation came to a sudden stop when Mother called, 'Estelle's waiting, Stacey.'

Estelle was the woman on lift duty for that week. Four mothers were involved in taking turns to pick up the children for school.

Stacey gave her another quick hug. 'See you Sunday arvie.'

Emma sighed. She too would have been racing down the passage to join the others. It hurt so much she had to wipe away the tears that welled up in her eyes. Even though the panic had now gone from her mind, she knew it would take a long time to adjust and accept what had happened to her. Tears again pricked maddeningly at her eyes and she angrily brushed them away with the backs of her hands. This constant crying has to stop. Determined not to cry, she clenched her teeth hard together. 'Time is a great healer,' Mom once told their neighbour when their little dog was killed. How much time, months, years, forever?

Father turned the car into a tree-lined drive leading off the main road. On a large wooden post on one side of the drive were the words, 'Happiness Inn' and on another post, 'The Sanctuary, Private Clinic.'

'I didn't know there was a private clinic out here as well!' exclaimed Mother, surprised. 'And it looks posh!' She laughed.

'You're right there,' replied Father, 'and very, very expensive.'

Emma was suddenly flooded with a sensation of alarm all the way to her fingertips. 'This is it,' she muttered, trying not to panic and to hold on to the belief that somehow everything would be all right, but it was no good. A scream welled up inside her and she didn't know if she could keep it in. She breathed in deeply to calm her body.

'What lovely surroundings!' Mother almost whispered.

Father turned to her and smiled. 'It's hard to believe all this is still in Johannesburg. It's like being in the country, far from civilization.'

All the old anger and antagonism flooded over Emma again and a hurt, like a rope tightening around her heart, almost suffocated her. She tried to say something but couldn't. Instead, she shrugged in a gesture of hopelessness and irritation and stared numbly at the surroundings.

They continued down the drive until they reached a turn where the trees came to an abrupt end. Ahead, surrounded by a two-meter high red brick wall, was a large rambling building with a red tiled roof. Driving through an open gateway, they passed the front of the building bordered on one side by a well-trimmed lawn with beds of flowers that were a profusion of colourful blooms.

'How enchanting!' Mother burst out, giving Emma a quick look over her shoulder.

Emma glanced casually about her. She was annoyed and wanted to snarl, 'Stop gushing for my benefit. I'm not impressed.' She had to bite her lip hard to stop the words from spilling out.

Father stopped the car in front of the entrance to the building and after he had fetched the wheelchair from the boot, settled her on the seat, he pushed her up a small ramp into the building.

Advancing towards them was a short, thin nurse with wiry brown hair sticking out from under her white cap. She gave them a welcoming smile. Emma nodded automatically. There was a terrible tight feeling in her chest. Then, suddenly, she felt surprisingly calm.

'Mr. and Mrs. du Preez?' the nurse queried, adding, 'and Emma?'

'Yes,' Father answered.

'Matron's expecting you. Please come with me.'

They followed her down a wide corridor and into an office. The matron, a white-haired, capable looking woman who had about her an unmistakable air of authority, was sitting at a desk. The office was small with a couple of pictures of groups of nurses hanging on the walls. As they entered Matron stood up and greeted them warmly.

'School's about to begin,' she said kindly. 'If you would say goodbye to Emma, Nurse McPherson can take her to the classroom.'

Emma stared dumbfounded at her. The suddenness of the parting brought tears to her eyes. She quickly took a deep breath and bit her trembling lips. Father, his face expressionless, bent down and kissed her, giving her a quick hug. Mother knelt down beside her. She looked as if she were about to burst into tears.

'We'll see you on Sunday afternoon,' she whispered, trying hard to keep her voice steady.

Emma, swallowing uncomfortably, nodded, her face strained and set. After Mother kissed her goodbye, Nurse McPherson wheeled her from the room.

'You'll enjoy your stay with us,' she said, cheerfully. 'We are a very happy family and you'll soon make friends.'

Emma moistened her lips to speak. At first no sound came. 'Yes, I'm sure,' she muttered, in a voice she couldn't recognize as her own. A spark of resentment grew within her and with it the bitterness came flooding back. She had to bite back the nasty words that were just itching to get out.

They entered another wide passageway that led to the classroom. She could hear the sound of voices and laughter.

Nurse McPherson pushed open a swing door, and Emma found herself in a large room full of children. A quick count revealed twenty boys and girls of various ages ranging from about twelve to eighteen years. Some were in wheelchairs sitting at a large table while others with irons on their legs, sat at desks. There was a general hubbub and for a while no one seemed to notice her. Gradually, one by one, they turned and looked at her. Some smiled and waved, others called out a greeting. A girl about her own age got up from her desk and walked unsteadily towards her. Her skin was a blotchy brown. She had a long thin face, prominent nose and straight, shoulder length lifeless-looking black hair and she wore a knee-length shapeless blue floral dress over her thin body. Her head and hands shook spasmodically in fact her whole body seemed to be uncoordinated.

'Hello!' greeted the girl, her voice quavering. 'You must be Emma, my new roommate. We've been expecting you.'

What, thought Emma, aghast. She stared at the girl whose mouth was slack and whose whole body twitched. Was she to share a room with her! Giving a little sniff, she tilted her nose heavenwards.

'Look after her, Elizabeth,' put in Nurse McPherson, and left.

'You can sit next to me,' Elizabeth invited, her face wreathed in smiles as she wheeled Emma to a table close to her desk.

'Do you always speak and walk so funny?' Emma asked, scowling.

'Yes,' she replied, quietly. 'I was born like this.'

'Who's being rude?' asked a boy, clearly irritated, who sat in a wheelchair at the table. He was about seventeen, thin and with a dark complexion. His thick black hair was closely cropped to his head. A red tartan blanket covered his legs. His large, dark restless penetrating eyes smoldering with annoyance, were boring into hers like lazer rays. She felt herself redden under his steady gaze.

'Elizabeth's a spastic, but that doesn't mean she's stupid,' he snapped. 'She's only sixteen and a computer whiz kid and will be writing her matric this year, that's more than a lot of able-bodied people can brag about.'

The atmosphere became frosty. He looked at her as if she had crawled out from under a stone, making her feel like some dumb kid. Blushing scarlet. She held her head high, glaring defiantly back at him.

Before she had time to reply, Elizabeth broke in, 'Emma, meet Ralph Masters. Don't be too hard on her, Ralph. I don't miss what I've never had, but it must be a shattering experience to suddenly lose the use of your legs.' As she spoke her head tilted uncontrollably swinging from side to side like a metronome and, for a brief fleeting moment, there came into her eyes a look of deep compassion.

Emma found herself burning with shame. With a great effort to keep her voice steady, for her mouth was dry, she muttered, 'I'm sorry, Elizabeth. That was rude of me and I'm truly sorry.' For the first time in her life she was ashamed of herself and wished she were someone else.

'I understand,' Elizabeth told her, patting her gently on the arm. 'This is Cindy,' she continued, pointing to a girl at the end of the table. She had short dark hair and was very plump, almost overflowing her wheelchair. 'The two boys opposite are Jackson and Ted and are only weekly boarders.'

Emma nodded.

Ted had bright ginger hair with a few freckles sprinkled over his nose. He called out, 'Hi!' Jackson nodded, but said nothing. His hair and eyes were dark and he looked surly.

Ralph's mouth quirked. 'I hope you are truly sorry,' he put in, scowling. 'Your nasty remark was uncalled for.'

Emma winced at the harshness in his voice and she looked sidelong at him. Their eyes locked. She looked away, her face flushing with humiliation.

He stared intently back at her studying her for a moment, his face full of curiosity. Suddenly recognition came into his eyes and he clapped a hand to his forehead and burst out laughing. 'Why, you're Emma du Preez, the Springbok gymnast!' He gaped at her in open admiration. 'You are one good gymnast.'

Emma felt herself recoil as if she had a punch in the stomach, colouring up to the roots of her hair, her green eyes flashed dangerously.

'Was,' she retorted. All she now had left were memories.

The door opened and the noise and laughter about them ceased.

'Good morning, Mr Webster,' chorused the children.

Emma stared in amazement at the thin bespectacled man in his early thirties, with a mop of thick black curly hair, who came hobbling into the classroom. He was encased in irons from his toes to just above his waist.

He smiled as he spoke. 'Good morning, children!' He had a gentle, sensitive voice. 'Are you rearing to go this morning?'

'Yes,' they chorused.

'We have a new student,' called Elizabeth, pointing to Emma. 'Meet Emma du Preez, Mr Webster.'

Emma turned scarlet.

'Welcome, Emma du Preez,' Mr Webster said warmly. 'I hope you'll be happy with us.'

All eyes were on her and she shifted uncomfortably in the wheelchair. 'Thanks,' she muttered, trying to smile, but her facial muscles had stiffened.

'We'll begin with a mental arithmetic competition,' he continued, 'A group versus B group. Get your thinking caps on.'

There were shouts of enthusiastic approval.

'Emma, you're in Group B,' he told her and turned to write a large A and B on the blackboard.

As he did so the chalk broke in two and one of the pieces fell to the floor.

Emma watched wide-eyed in astonishment and disbelief as Mr. Webster loosened the nuts on either side of his waist irons, automatically sending the top part of his body falling forward. He retrieved the chalk and gripping the table for support slowly eased to an upright position and re-fastened the bolts to keep his body straight. He continued to write on the board.

Emma looked around the class. No one seemed to think that Mr Webster's gyrations were at all strange, but waited expectantly for the questions.

Emma found herself as excited as the other children when she knew the answers to some of the questions and eagerly put up her hand. This went on for some fifteen minutes and she was sorry when it came to an end.

After the competition he announced. 'Now it's time for a little shorthand for the six seniors. The rest of you take out your readers and study the next two chapters for a comprehension test.

Emma was surprised to find the shorthand lesson absorbing. All those squiggles were words and they fascinated her. After the lesson Elizabeth pushed her to a long table standing against the far-side wall of the room. On it were enough computers and manuals for all the senior students. She had a slight knowledge of the Microsoft word program so she found it easy to follow. Elizabeth was a great help and Emma remembered Ralph saying she was a computer whiz kid.

While they were typing, Mr. Webster spent time with the other scholars.

English and History came next and all too soon Mr Webster announced, 'School's over for today. I'll see you at nine-thirty tomorrow morning.' After saying goodbye he left the room.

The children who were in calipers and able to walk pushed those in wheelchairs from the room. Elizabeth came up to Emma. 'Before we go for lunch I'll show you our room.'

Just then Ralph wheeled up to them. 'I challenge you to a game of 'Trivial Pursuit', he said, grinning.

'Don't take him on, Emma,' Elizabeth warned, 'That is where he's a whiz kid and no one has ever been able to beat him. Not even the nurses.'

He laughed. 'Spoil sport, Elizabeth. Remember, the more you play the more you learn.' Chuckling, he wheeled himself away at break neck speed.

Elizabeth pushed Emma out of the classroom and down the corridor.

Emma was astonished at how calmly she had accepted her new home, feeling completely at ease in her new surroundings.

'Ralph's so wild in his chair,' Elizabeth told her. 'How he manages to get from one place to the other without an accident I'll never know.'

By this time Ralph was nearing the end of the corridor and almost collided with Matron as she came round the corner. 'Ralph,' she remonstrated, 'I've told you so often before not to practice for the wheelchair Olympics in the corridors. You're going to hurt someone.'

'Sorry, Mam,' Emma heard him call as he hastened headlong on his way.

Matron shook her head, but there was a smile on her face. When she saw Emma she came up to her and asked, 'Well, Emma, how did you enjoy your first day at school?'

'Fine thanks,' she replied.

'Good, I'm glad to hear that.' Matron turned to Elizabeth. 'You can show Emma around.'

'Yes, Mam,' Elizabeth replied cheerfully. 'I'm taking her to our room first.'

Matron smiled and nodded, walking on.

A mirror was fixed to the wall at the far end of the corridor. Emma glanced in it as they drew near. By normal standards Elizabeth was ugly. Her shoulder length black straight hair was lank and lifeless and her blotched face gruesome. She had an ungainly walk and her body twitched spasmodically. But nonetheless there was about her an unmistakable dignity.

No doubt others had remarked about her slurred speech and the way she walked. Emma winced when she remembered Elizabeth replying simply after her rude remark, 'Yes, I was born like this.' There had been no self-pity or resentment in her voice, just a plain statement of fact that the genie within her had been there from the very beginning, denying her even the briefest freedom to move and speak without hindrance.

In her compassion, Elizabeth had said she didn't miss something that had never been hers to enjoy. Whilst Emma supposed this may be true, in the opposite sense she at least could look back with pleasure and pride at what she had achieved.

As they progressed down the corridor she was forced, in spite of herself, to admit that not only Elizabeth, but Mr. Webster and the other children too, had had a profound effect on her. The teacher had to loosen bolts to perform the simple act of picking up a piece of chalk and the chatter and laughter could have come from any classroom at a normal school.

Once again she looked into the mirror. Elizabeth intently pushed her along as if it were the only thing in the world that mattered. She looked at herself, Emma du Preez, who had once been a Springbok gymnast, but was now being pushed along by an ungainly girl. A girl who had somehow found within herself the means of coming face to face with the uncaring genie that had taken possession of her body, but had left her gracious mind untouched.

On an impulse, she looked up at Elizabeth and gently patted her hand. 'I'm glad you're my friend,' she said, a little self-consciously.

Elizabeth smiled radiantly down at her.

Half way down the next corridor and on the left, Elizabeth pushed open a door and wheeled Emma into their bedroom.

'This is lovely,' Emma gasped. 'Built in cupboards, dressing table come writing bureau. I suppose the three drawers on the right will be mine?'

'Yes, that's my bed below the window,' Elizabeth came in.

'I can do with a smaller mirror above the desk,' Emma moaned. 'I don't enjoy looking at a life size picture of myself in a wheelchair.' She laughed. 'But I do like the duvets and matching curtains. Purple and white stripes are so cool.'

She felt a strange sensation that something in her life had ended, but something else had just begun.

****

CHAPTER FIVE

Tough Love

The next few days passed at an astonishing speed and Emma had to grudgingly admit that there was so much that was interesting in her new surroundings, and what was more astonishing, she loved it.

They were awakened at six each morning and, after donning bathing costumes, with the assistance of the nurses, were taken to the gymnasium. It contained a shallow, heated pool and various forms of exercise equipment. Not bad, she thought. The arm exerciser machine was something her coach had spoken about and hoped to get one day for the school. Then she noticed the parallel bar in the corner. There, children who had recently been fitted with calipers practiced walking in them. The doctor had mentioned that one-day she may be able to walk with the aid of calipers and she dearly hoped it would be so.

Emma was placed on a broad step leading down into the pool and, under the guidance of the therapist, exercised first her legs, by pulling them up and down with her hands, and then she exercised her shoulders and arms. She was surprised to discover how easy and effortless the exercises were to do in the water. After exercising, they had a bath, breakfasted, and went to school.

Emma thought back to the first morning at therapy. She happened to glance at Ralph who was climbing into the water and was horrified to see his legs. They were about the size of a child of three. Immediately their eyes met, Ralph averted his gaze and it came to her with an almost sickening realization that she now understood why he always kept his legs covered with a blanket.

Collecting her thoughts she had waved and called out, 'Hello, Ralph.'

At first he ignored her and then slowly the look of embarrassment that had clouded his face changed into what could have been a smile as he acknowledged her wave. Holding on to the rail that bordered the pool, he began jumping up and down with such energy it made her tired to look at him. Did he have to attack everything he did with such exuberance, she wondered?

Elizabeth came and sat beside her.

'What happened to Ralph?' Emma asked.

Elizabeth stared at her uncomprehendingly for a moment before understanding came to her. 'Oh, you mean his legs?' she said, 'Polio.'

'Polio!' Emma exclaimed, 'I thought it had died out many years ago.'

'No, not altogether. Ralph lived with his grandmother in a small rural township far from the nearest town. His mother had abandoned him and he was never immunized as a baby. At five years he contracted polio and it was some days before he was taken to a doctor. He almost died.' Elizabeth shook her head sadly. 'His chest is still weak and he often suffers from asthma attacks which seem to be getting worse instead of better, and sometimes he has to spend a night in an oxygen tent.'

'Where's his grandmother now?' Emma wanted to know.

'She died about six years ago. He never mentions her. I believe she visited him a couple of times when he first arrived here, some eleven years ago. He's never seen his mother.'

Emma wondered whether his restlessness and zest for life was his way of trying to blot out memories of the past. She fell silent for a few moments and then asked, 'Where can we find a game of 'Trivial Pursuit'?'

'I have one,' Elizabeth answered.

'Good. I have a plan.'

Elizabeth looked at her in surprise.

'We must learn all the questions and answers,' Emma explained.

'But there are thousands,' groaned Elizabeth.

'I know, but if we share them we'll manage. At least we'll be able to learn a large load of questions, maybe enough to win the game.'

'Why?'

'I want us to challenge Ralph to a game. This time he won't win. We'll make sure of that.'

Elizabeth gasped. Then she chuckled. 'You devious little monkey! Yes, I'm sure we can.'

'We'll study every spare minute,' Emma continued, 'It shouldn't take us too long to memorize the questions and answers. Your memory's particularly good, Elizabeth, far better than mine.'

Elizabeth laughed. 'Flattery will get you everywhere.'

Emma felt a thrill of excitement rising up in her. From that day onwards she refused to be wheeled around and after an initial struggle managed to propel herself to wherever she wanted to go.

This was not difficult for the building was designed for the handicapped. There were no stairs, only ramps, and all the doorways were wide enough to allow wheelchairs of all shapes and sizes to pass through.

It wasn't long before she was able to keep up with Ralph and she beamed with satisfaction when, one afternoon, she overtook him in the corridor. At first he was taken aback, but when he had overcome his surprise, he burst out laughing. 'Clever girl. I'll have to rev up my wheelchair.'

Emma felt a blush rise to her cheeks. 'One of these days I'll challenge you to a race,' she retorted. Tilting her chin defiantly and with Ralph's laughter echoing in her ears, she went in search of Elizabeth.

The first Sunday her parents and Stacey were about to arrive, Emma waited in a state of excitement in the enclosed verandah on the side of the building facing the clinic. There were a few younger children also waiting for their visitors. She saw the car drive in and park. Her parents and Stacey, carrying a large packet, climbed out of the car. They were laughing as the three of them walked towards the building. Then her mother put her arms around Stacey and gave her a quick hug.

Emma watched this show of affection and something seemed to snap inside her and a feeling of envy or jealousy, the green-eyed monster her mother called it, took over her whole being. She realized with horror that she was missing out on the close family relationship she had always taken for granted. There had never been any sibling rivalry in the home as both girls excelled in the work they did, Stacey in her schoolwork and she at gymnastics and they knew that their parents were proud of them both. Now she was out of it all, a stranger. Envy and jealousy was a new feeling she didn't know she had and didn't like it, but somehow it had come to stay.

When her parents and Stacey arrived they must have sensed the tension in her and the smiles on their faces froze. They looked at her tentatively and went to sit down at a table at the far end of the room.

Stacey handed her the packet. 'This is a large card signed by all your school mates,' she said.

Emma took it and threw it on the table. 'Thanks,' she muttered.

'Matron has told us how well you've settled in,' Mother said, trying to smile, but it twisted into a grimace.

'And I suppose that's eased your conscience for kicking me out of the house,' Emma spat out. Suddenly she wished with all her heart that she could swallow back the words when she saw the smile fade from Mother's face and the way she tried to fight back the tears threatening to spill down her cheeks.

'I didn't mean to say those cruel things,' she wanted to shout, but an uncontrollable rebelliousness seemed to force her to keep quiet. Instead, she just looked down at the floor.

Father was angry, very angry. She could see it from the firmness of his jaw and the way his eyes flashed. Yet he continued to talk lightheartedly to her. It was only when it was time for them to leave that he said quietly, almost in a whisper, 'Emma, our visit seems to have upset you. We'll stay away for two or three weeks, or until you're ready to be civil. Matron can contact us.' His mouth was tense and there was a muscle twitching in his jaw.

Immediately the blood rushed to her face and a sense of panic threatened to overwhelm her. She heard a faint gasp from Mother.

Father's words stung her like a whiplash and a terrible chill ran through her. For a moment she was too stunned to reply. Her mouth suddenly became dry as dust and her tongue clung to her palate. She stared at him in horror. But he can't do that after all she's been through.

Mother and Stacey said hurried good-byes and left.

Father was about to follow when Emma called out, 'Please, don't leave like this, Dad. I'm sorry, truly sorry. I can't seem to stop myself from being nasty. It's like someone else has taken control of me and there's nothing I can do about it.'

'I'm sorry too, Emma. But until you are able to control that someone else, we'll stay away.'

'But you can't,' she cried, her voice shrill. 'You have to visit, please, Father. I'll die if you don't visit. I promise to do my best not to be nasty again.'

Father looked squarely at her, his face solemn. 'You'll have to do better than that, my girl. I'm not only doing this for your sake, but for Mother's and Stacey's too. It's no fun to have their Sunday afternoons spoilt.'

She panicked and her stomach tightened in a knot of fear. She remembered her crying spells in hospital when Father issued a similar ultimatum. But this time it seemed more serious. Father had obviously made up his mind. What could she do to change it? She would truly die if she didn't see them every week. 'Please give me one more chance,' she pleaded, 'just one. You won't be sorry if you do.'

An uneasy silence followed. Father bit his lip and frowned. Emma held her breath and her heart beat thundered in her ears. Please say yes, she prayed. Don't torture me like this.

Finally, Father broke the silence. 'All right, Emma, your last chance. Please don't let me down.'

She smiled in relief. 'Oh, thank you. Thank you. You won't be sorry, Father. I promise you that.'

Father kissed her goodbye and left. She watched his departing figure and wished with all her heart that she could turn back the clock and start the afternoon all over again. But, alas, it was too late.

'What's wrong with me?' she cried. 'Why do I get so gross?' She rubbed her forehead hard. 'I suppose jealousy is making me nasty because they all look so happy and fit and healthy, AND THEY CAN WALK!' She scowled. 'But it's not their fault that I can't,' she reasoned. 'I'm just being spiteful.'

She didn't know how long she sat there deep in thought when she heard a voice call.

It was Elizabeth. 'It's almost supper time.'

Emma burst into tears.

'What's up?' queried Elizabeth.

Emma gave a low stifled moan. 'I've been so ugly to everyone this afternoon,' she sobbed and haltingly told Elizabeth the whole story. 'Why am I so nasty to the people who love me? I can't seem to stop myself.'

Elizabeth was silent for a few seconds, then she smiled. 'Your father's practicing tough love and it usually works.'

Emma frowned. 'What's tough love?'

'It's a philosophy to remind children that parents are people too and that they have the right to stop their children from wrecking their lives.'

Emma blushed. 'Oh, Elizabeth, I've been so wrapped up in my own misery. I know my parents and even Stacey have been going through a difficult time. Our whole world has been turned topsy-turvy. Because I'm hurting so much I've tried to get it out on them.'

'As long as you accept this you've won the battle,' Elizabeth said softly, and gave Emma a quick hug.

But that wasn't to be the end of Emma's trouble for later that evening she was surprised when Ralph was rude to her. It happened when leaving the room after supper. She accidentally bumped into his chair.

'Hey, watch where you're going, Moron!' he exclaimed, his face grim.

Puzzled, she glanced at him. Then anger rose up in her when she realized he wasn't fooling. 'Who rattled your cage,' she snapped.

'Stop bugging me, spoiled brat!' he retorted and wheeled himself away.

'What's his problem?' she muttered, biting her lip, confused at his outburst, hard to believe the change in him. A dull flush of colour spread in her cheeks. 'Get lost, Ralph Masters,' she snapped.

The next day Ralph avoided her and Elizabeth.

'What's up with him?' she asked Elizabeth.

'Oh, that! He's going through another identity crisis, he calls it.' She laughed. 'Every now and again he gets depressed and crawls into his shell. It's best to leave him alone until he surfaces. He'll soon be his old self again. Give him space.'

'In other words he's just plain moody and rude,' Emma offered, biting her lip. 'I've been a pain too so should understand.'

'It's not like him to be rude,' Elizabeth came back, frowning, and added, 'We all have our off days. I call it being 'bossies', getting a bit mad in the head at times.' She chuckled. 'The word comes from my Afrikaans ancestry.'

In the television lounge later that evening, Ralph came in and sheepishly wheeled himself beside Emma. She avoided him. He mustn't think he can snarl at me one minute and be nice the next as though nothing has happened, she thought. I'm not going to put up with his moods.

No one said anything. Emma couldn't concentrate on the film. She could sense Ralph was trying to say something and she kept her face averted from him. Later she gave him a quick glance. For a fleeting moment something about the way he looked, so forlorn, touched her deeply. He reminded her of a lost puppy in a pet shop. Suddenly it all seemed so ridiculous and she had to stifle an absurd desire to giggle. To break the tension she said the first thing that came into her head. 'All right, what's bugging you, Mr Moody Ralph Masters?'

'I'm sorry I was a pain,' he whispered, so as not to be overheard. 'I had a bit of nasty news, but that's no excuse. Put it down to my age. Teenagers are usually scrambled eggs, in other words crazy mixed up kids, and I'm going through my gloom and doom phase.'

'Speak for yourself,' she whispered back, smiling. After all she had no right to judge him. Hadn't she gone through a spell of gloom herself, a long spell?

His white teeth flashed into a grin. And there was a glow in his face.

She grinned back. It was like a magic moment, she thought, surprised at herself.

The following afternoon she and Elizabeth were in their room. They had spent some of the afternoon studying the 'Trivial Pursuit' questions and answers and were excited with their progress, delighted to discover that they knew quite a few answers without having to refer to the cards.

Emma giggled. 'We are clever, my mate. Some of the answers are so obvious that I think they can't possibly be correct. Yebo! Ralph Masters, you are going to get the surprise of your life.'

'Yes,' agreed Elizabeth, her eyes dancing mischievously. 'I can't wait to challenge him. When you first suggested it I thought you were crazy, but since getting down to the questions I know we can do it.'

'Give us another week and we'll be almost perfect.' Emma told her confidently. 'So maybe the following week we can send out the challenge.'

Elizabeth grimaced and Emma laughed.

After studying for another thirty minutes Elizabeth said with a sigh, 'My brain's tired and my bum's numb. I'm going for a walk. It is such a lovely day, Emma, please come with me.'

'No thanks. I'll see you later.'

Elizabeth left the room. Emma glanced through a few more questions and then decided to go to the rumpus room to watch the sport on television. She still had an occasional twitch of sadness and longing when a program on gymnastics came on, but it was getting better.

She wheeled herself out of the room and along the corridor. As she passed the bedroom that Ralph shared with the other two boys she thought she heard a cry for help. It cannot be. My ears must be playing tricks with me. Puzzled, she stopped and listened. There it was again.

'Help me! Help me!'

****

CHAPTER SIX

The Koppie

Without hesitating, Emma turned the knob, flung open the door and rushed in. She gasped! Ralph was sitting at a desk on which stood a microphone. A book lay open in front of him.

'I'm...I'm..I'm sorry,' she stammered, red-faced and apologetic. 'I never meant...I thought you were in trouble.' She was unable to continue.

Ralph stared at her in disbelief. His eyes widened and a flicker of laughter crossed his face. He said teasingly, 'Tell me, what trouble can I get into here? I wish I could be so lucky!' He grinned broadly.

She flushed angrily. Why does he always have to laugh at me, wishing a hole would open up in the floor and swallow her, 'I thought you were shouting for help,' she said defensively, staring icily at him.

'I'm reading a children's story for Tape Aids for the Blind,' he explained. 'Now I'll have to begin the chapter again.' His tone was not a rebuke, but one of amusement, as a smile played around the corners of his mouth. 'It's comforting to know that you would have helped me if I was in trouble.'

Embarrassed, Emma took a moment or two before replying, 'What would you have done if you heard someone shouting for help? I haven't X-ray eyes.' Then a flash of curiosity came over her. Staring at him inquisitively, and on an impulse, she asked, tentatively, 'If I remain very quiet may I stay and listen?'

He hesitated for a moment, scratching his chin thoughtfully, and then nodded. 'Sure. Do you mind closing the door, Emma?'

Willingly she complied and sat quietly while he ran the tape back and began to read. She became enthralled as she listened to him changing his voice for each character in the story and gesticulating with his hands to give added emphasis to the words, now and again pausing for dramatic effect. She could hear the authority in his tone and he was so consumed with his task that he seemed to be oblivious to everything around him, even her presence was completely forgotten.

When he had finished the chapter he switched off the recorder and gave her a broad grin.

A spark ignited inside her and she warmed towards him, exclaiming eagerly, 'Oh, Ralph, you have a beautiful voice. You should take up acting. You live each part of the story like a true actor.'

Ralph stared at her, his eyes black and shiny, then he burst out laughing. 'Imagine this,' he said, trying to control his mirth, 'Here we have Ralph Masters revving up his wheelchair. He's taking off and rushing across the stage to rescue the damsel in distress. Oh no, wait for it, the wheelchair's skidding out of control. Watch out! It's flown into the wings. There's a loud kaplonk, followed by a scream. A few minutes later we see the hero carried on to the stage. His broken body, curled up like a pretzel, is laid on a couch. 'I must save her,' he gasps, coughing wheezily, and then his head suddenly falls to one side. The curtain closes and the audience is silent for a moment, before the theatre rocks with the volume of applause.'

For a second Emma felt like hitting him. 'Stop it, Ralph! I'm serious. Stage acting isn't the only kind of acting in the world. There's such a thing as radio.'

Ralph looked at her curiously and then slowly nodded. 'You may have something there.'

Encouraged, she added, 'You could also be a newsreader on TV. All they do is sit at a table. You never see the whole of them. I read in one of these TV magazines that the men only wear formal clothing on top and sit in worn out jeans or sloppy tracksuit bottoms or running shorts.'

His eyes twinkled and he gave a theatrical sigh. 'My options are improving by the minute.'

Ignoring his remark she said softly, 'I'd love to read stories for the blind. Do you think I'll be able to do it too?'

For the first time since they met the cool amusement that was invariably in his eyes was missing. He looked at her steadily and his large dark eyes were tender. A sudden shyness came over her and she lowered her head.

He answered quietly, 'Why not give it a try? I'll help you. It's not as easy as it seems. I have to do a lot of practicing before I record. The most difficult part is changing my voice and to make sure I keep to the same voice for each character.'

'I'll practice and practice,' she promised.

'Right!' He took a book from the desk and offered it to her. 'Here's a short story for small children. Practice reading it out aloud and then come back to me when you're ready.'

Emma took the book and after mumbling her thanks hurried back to her room and excitedly began reading it out loud, stumbling at first, then gradually being able to control her voice. There were only two characters involved.

A while later Elizabeth came to remind her that the tea bell had rung ten minutes ago.

'There's cheese cake on the menu,' she said, rubbing her stomach.

'Oh, cool! I can't miss that!' Emma exclaimed. 'It's my favourite. I'm sure I can eat a whole plateful on my own.'

When they were having tea, Elizabeth, somewhat to Emma's surprise bent over and whispered secretively, grinning all over her face. 'I've found a lovely hideaway in the veld, on top of a small koppie.'

'On top of a koppie!' Emma gasped. 'But there are no koppies near here! They are all many kilometers away.'

'Shshshsh!' Elizabeth warned, 'That's what you think. On one side of the building, next to the garages and storerooms, there's a large hole in the fence. I slipped through the hole earlier this afternoon and wandered about the veld and came across a path that led me to this koppie. It's not far. We can't see it from here because it's hidden behind the buildings. The path is almost smooth. I'm sure it's good enough for a wheelchair. All we have to do is follow it and it will lead us to the koppie. I went up the koppie to check and the path too is also fairly smooth. Interested?'

'I'm interested, but I'll never be able to climb a koppie,' protested Emma, 'especially with wheels.'

'It's not all that steep and I'll push you. Oh come on now, Emma, where's your sense of adventure? You'll enjoy the change.'

Emma laughed. 'You're right there.' Elizabeth had sparked an adventurous response in her.

Later that afternoon Elizabeth could be found pushing Emma towards the outbuildings.

The wheelchair clacked along a brick path. Just their luck the grounds and buildings were deserted. Emma chuckled delightedly and turned to look conspiratorially at Elizabeth, who was smiling broadly.

'Like mischievous elves we are,' Emma whispered, laughing. She had to admit that she felt excited and yet a little scared.

Elizabeth, with eyes sparkling, face animated, grinned at her without replying.

They came to the hole in the fence and after ducking to avoid a strand of barbed wire, found themselves on the other side of the world, or so it seemed. Everywhere was stillness and tranquillity.

The sudden change of scenery made Emma gasp with delight. 'This is great!'

The vast expanse of veld, that seemed to go on forever, was dotted with clumps of grass and an occasional thorn tree. In the far distance was a misty range of Blue Mountains, they weren't really blue, of course, they only looked blue because of the shadow.

They followed a well-worn gravel path for about two hundred meters until they passed through a cluster of trees and reached the bottom of a small koppie.

Emma laughed. 'It's a koppie all right and not very large.' She glanced apprehensively at the stony path leading almost all the way to the top. 'It's not as easy as it looks.' She bit her lip thoughtfully. 'I don't think we're going to make it,' she added doubtfully. 'It's too rough and stony and these wheels are not made for climbing. I can't think why you thought they were.'

'If you believe in something with all your heart you can make it happen,' replied Elizabeth confidently. 'And I believe we can do it. Also, we haven't come all this way to give up now and you'll love it up there.'

Emma sighed. 'All right, you win. Let's give it a bash.'

It was with great difficulty that they eventually reached the top. Perspiration was running down their faces, Emma's a bright red. After catching their breath, they looked at each other and burst out laughing.

'Talk about a couple of nitwits! Do you think it has been worth it?' Elizabeth asked, still gasping for breath.

Emma clapped her hands. 'Yes, definitely,' she agreed, as she looked about her approvingly. The rugged beauty of the valley and the misty Blue Mountains almost took one's breath away. 'It's awesome, as our American cousins would say.'

'It'll be easier going down,' Elizabeth promised.

Little did she know!

The peace and calm of their surroundings spread over them. Swallows darted across the hillside, bees buzzed around some wild flowers, a few butterflies wavered aimlessly about and a dragon fly, its glittering, transparent wings flashed low around them and then disappeared. Birds twittered amongst the clumps of grass that seemed to whisper in a slight breeze that blew across them. They could also hear the boring, monotonous cooing of pigeons.

Elizabeth pushed Emma into the shade of a gnarled and twisted branch of a thorn tree growing nearby and sat down on a rock beside her. The atmosphere of tranquility enveloped them and with the scents of the veld mingling in the air, for a brief moment, Emma felt a wonderful awareness of just being alive. Somehow, sitting on the top of the koppie, her crippled legs didn't seem to matter.

'Nothing is important up here except the beauty of our surroundings,' Elizabeth said softly.

Emma nodded. She knew exactly what she meant.

They sat there not saying anything. It was so relaxing gazing into the distance. In-between the expanse of veld lay farmland where cattle grazed. They could hear the lonely haunting sound of a tractor as it made its way across the fields and a cow mooed sadly. All around them grasshoppers and lizards darted about. White clouds rolled lazily across the blue sky. The leafy tops of the trees hardly stirred as a gentle breeze passed over the veld and an aeroplane, like a toy, flew high above them.

Emma broke the silence. 'Ralph is a strange person, isn't he?' she asked as if she couldn't care less.

'No stranger than anyone else here,' Elizabeth assured her.

Emma thought she sensed a note of annoyance in her voice and she breathed in deeply, a little irritated. 'Then it's because he doesn't like me that everything I say seems to amuse him. He makes me feel like a real twit!'

Elizabeth didn't answer for a moment. There was a faraway look of concentration in her eyes. Then, 'Believe me when I tell you that he likes you more than you realize.'

'How can you tell?'

'I've known Ralph for a long time. He and I have been here the longest. Take it from me he's fond of you.'

Emma was curious. 'Did he say something?'

'He doesn't have to.'

Emma laughed. 'Madam Elizabeth, Queen of the Horriescopes.'

Elizabeth didn't respond and Emma gazed intently at her. 'Something wrong, Elizabeth?' she asked, alarmed.

Elizabeth sighed deeply. 'No, not really wrong. It's just…there are times when I hate the way I am and want so desperately to be normal.' A glimmer of hurt flickered in her eyes. She sighed again and gave Emma a rather wan half-smile. 'I'm usually able to work through my gloom, but sometimes it eats into me. That's why I can identify with Ralph's black moods.'

Emma was startled by her outburst. 'You're a beautiful person, Elizabeth, and the best friend I've ever had.' She bit her lip thoughtfully before continuing, 'The only friend I've ever had. Gymnastics took up all my time.'

Emma heard Elizabeth's sharp intake of breath. 'Beautiful person? Isn't that a contradiction? I think it's by time you had some reading glasses.'

'I'm not talking about your physical body,' Emma hastened to reply, and then bit her lip in embarrassment.

Elizabeth gave her a sheepish grin. 'I know what you mean, but a perfect body would help.'

'You're telling me!'

Then like a bolt from the blue it came to Emma that Elizabeth liked Ralph more than just a friend. Elizabeth's mouth twitched violently. Emma knew this could be either in amusement or anger and waited with bated breath. She hoped she hadn't hurt Elizabeth in any way.

Elizabeth's face brightened. 'How did we become so philosophical? It's not right to be morbid on a beautiful clear day such as this with a wonderful view to feast our tired eyes on.' She laughed. 'This is a place where we can drift and dream of being somewhere else, our escape from the real world.'

Emma, relieved, said tongue in cheek, 'You're right there, but feast our tired eyes on? Really, Elizabeth, what type of books have you been reading?'

Before she knew it they were laughing together and it felt wonderful. Elizabeth was such fun to be with, Emma thought fondly, and she had the gift of making one feel special. Suddenly she cried out excitedly, pointing to a bush a few meters away. 'Oh look, wild berries. I don't know the name, but I know the berry. They're edible and delicious.'

'I'll get some for you,' suggested Elizabeth as she jumped up and ran to the bush.

'Watch out!' Emma shouted.

But she was too late. Elizabeth tripped on a large stone, missed her footing, and toppled backwards, out of sight.

Emma heard a short breathless cry and a thud, then silence.

****

CHAPTER SEVEN

Where's Ralph?

'Elizabeth!' yelled Emma.

'I'm all right,' Elizabeth's shaky voice came floating up to her.

Relieved, Emma moved slowly to the edge. Straining her neck forward and hanging on to the wheels of the chair so that it wouldn't slip, she stretched out her neck and peered down. The hairs on her arms rose in horror.

It was as though a giant bulldozer had raked the side of the koppie, leaving in its wake an almost smooth area of rock that dropped vertically for some hundred or so meters to the bottom. About two meters down a wide ledge extended horizontally across it. Elizabeth, miraculously, was sitting on the ledge directly below her. Emma knew there was no way Elizabeth could ever safely leave her refuge without assistance.

'Elizabeth!' she called softly.

Elizabeth looked up and gave her a feeble wave.

Emma shouted encouragingly. 'I'll go for help.'

'O K, but do please be quick. I don't like heights,' came Elizabeth's tremulous reply. 'It's scary down here.'

'I'll be as fast as I can,' Emma promised, trying her utmost to keep her voice steady for it felt like a lot of insect wings were beating wildly inside her stomach, all trying to escape.

Reversing the wheelchair slightly, she turned and began making her way back over the uneven ground. The wheelchair jerked uncomfortably as it skidded and bumped down the incline.

'Elizabeth said it would be easier going down,' she grunted. 'How wrong. I can hardly keep control and I don't want my fingers to get caught in the spokes.'

When she came to a sharp turn she realized, too late, that there was a steep slope immediately ahead of her. She vaguely remembered the difficulty she and Elizabeth had experienced ascending it. If it wasn't for Elizabeth's keenness to get to the top she would have suggested they turn back immediately.

A cry escaped from her when the wheelchair suddenly swerved violently and lurched forward before gathering speed. She clung desperately to the arms of the chair as, completely out of control, it hurtled on its way. When she had almost reached the bottom, she felt a jolt as the wheelchair hit a large stone. In that instant, she was flung out. Unable to stop, she rolled down the rest of the way, coming to a halt against a clump of grass at the bottom.

'Eina,' she groaned.

She tried to scream, but no sound left her throat. Dazed and dizzy she stared vaguely about her. Slowly her brain cleared. Her head ached and her body felt as if it had gone through a mangle. For a moment she lay still, going over in her mind what had happened before raising her head and looking about her.

Dusk was gathering fast. Cicadas began to sing in a nearby tree. It was then she remembered Elizabeth. In alarm she painfully pulled herself up into a sitting position. She saw the wheelchair lying on its side against a small thorn tree, about ten meters away.

'I must get to it,' she muttered. 'I'm too far away for anyone to hear my screams for help.'

Leaning heavily on her arms she slowly dragged herself over the uneven ground until, gasping for breath, she finally reached the wheelchair. Her arms and hands were bruised. Large tears were gaping on the knees of her jeans and her shoulders ached something awful.

'Ooogh,' she moaned. 'I'm so sore.'

After resting for a moment to catch her breath she clutched at the arms of the wheelchair and locked the brakes. Several attempts later, she managed to get it in an upright position. But try as she may she wasn't able to climb into it because every time she grasped hold of the arms to pull herself on to the seat, it skidded away.

She lay on the ground listening to the veld noises. There was the occasional croak of a frog and the crickets and other insects were trying to out-sing one another. The raucous screech of a hadidah echoed all around her. In the stillness every sound was magnified. Looking up into the tree she noticed a movement in the upper branches. An owl screeched down at her, it's eyes two pinpricks of light in the gathering darkness.

'Oh go away!' she said crossly.

As if in response, the owl, with a flutter of wings, left the branch and disappeared into the night.

By this time Emma was desperate. She had to get help for Elizabeth. She noticed that the lowest branch of the tree reached out across the wheelchair. The trunk, she thought excitedly, if I grab hold of it I could pull myself up and grasp the branch. 'This is where my experience as a gymnast can come in handy. My therapy exercises have strengthened my arms so I'm sure they'll take my weight. Then I can lower myself carefully into the chair.'

Placing her arms around the narrow trunk and with great effort, she managed to pull herself upright. 'So far so good,' she gasped. 'My muscles are not as good as they were in my gymnastic days but they're not too bad.' Breathing heavily, she took hold of the branch first with one hand and then with the other and pulled herself along. Her body felt as though it weighed a ton and her legs dangled like two lumps of lead. It took all her strength to hold on to the branch. Finally, she was above the wheelchair and about to lower herself onto the seat, when there was a loud 'snap!'

The branch broke and she fell heavily into the chair. It swayed dangerously for a moment or two, but by quickly shifting her weight from one side to the other she was able to prevent it from toppling over.

Heaving a sigh of relief, she wheeled herself slowly and without further incident to the hole in the fence. Once back in the grounds she took a panicky look around to search for help, but saw no one. In desperation, she shouted, 'Help! Help!'

Immediately, running feet and answering calls responded to her cries.

Matron, followed by Nurse McPherson, made their way quickly towards her. Behind them she saw Ralph.

'Where have you been, my dear? We've been looking all over for you!' Matron exclaimed, 'and where's Elizabeth?'

After Emma had given a brief explanation of what had happened, Matron turned to Nurse McPherson, 'Take care of her while I arrange for Elizabeth to be rescued.' She hurried into the building.

Ralph looked at Emma's scratched arms and hands and the large tears in her jeans and then at her. Something that could have been relief lighted briefly in his eyes.

'Are you O K?' he asked, unsteadily.

Why, he must have been worried about me, Emma thought, blushing scarlet when she remembered what Elizabeth had told her.

'Yes, I'm fine,' she assured him.

He flashed her a dazzling smile.

'I must get her to the sick bay immediately for a check up before Dr Stephenson leaves,' broke in Nurse McPherson. 'You can talk to her tomorrow, Ralph.'

He nodded.

At the sick bay Dr Stephenson examined Emma. He was a large man with a potbelly and a double chin. When he laughed, and that was often, his chins all joined in. 'Well, well,' he said, chuckling, 'Except for the bruises and scratches, you're none the worse after your ordeal. You're a lucky girl.'

After a bath, Nurse McPherson rubbed some soothing ointment into her scratches and she was put to bed.

A maid brought her supper but Emma just stared disinterestedly at it. She wished Elizabeth was back and hoped nothing had happened to her. A sudden tiredness spread over her and she felt empty and very lonely. She realized in some amazement that she hadn't been lonely since arriving at the school.

Listlessly, she stabbed the fork into a small potato before resting it on the side of the plate. Then, to her great delight, Elizabeth was wheeled into the room. She jumped from the chair. 'Thanks, Mary, I'm fine now,' she told the young nurse's aid.

'All right, Elizabeth. Hi Emma!' Mary greeted.

'Hi!' Emma responded.

'See you tomorrow,' she called as she left the room.

'Oh, Elizabeth, I'm so glad to see you,' cried Emma, studying her carefully. 'You look fine.' Shuddering, she added, 'If that ledge hadn't been there,' she stopped and clicked her tongue angrily, 'But it was and that's that.'

Elizabeth laughed. 'I've just come from the sick bay and believe it or not, I only have a bump on my head and a few scratches. I've been so lucky.' She ran her tongue around her lips and added, 'We've both been so lucky.'

Emma nodded.

Matron walked briskly into the room. She shook her head and wagged her finger at them. 'In future you must not leave the grounds,' she scolded. She seemed to deliberately speak slowly as if she wanted to make sure that every word would sink in. 'As you have both no doubt discovered, it isn't safe for you to wander off on your own.'

'We're sorry,' Emma told her, contrite.

'Yes,' put in Elizabeth.

'I'm sure you are.' Still shaking her head she left the room.

'What happened?' prompted Emma, her tiredness forgotten. 'How were you rescued?'

Elizabeth gave a half sigh. 'After you left I was scared stiff, but I knew you'd get help.'

'I nearly didn't make it,' broke in Emma and related her tale.

'Wow! No wonder it seemed as if you'd gone forever!'

'How were you finally brought up from the ledge?' Emma was curious to know.

'Old Joshua, the gardener, tied a rope around the thorn tree and lowered himself down. His son, Silas, flashed a torch to light up his way. By this time it was very dark. There wasn't even a moon! I was terrified, but Joshua tied the other end of the rope around me and I was pulled up. It was 'eina', I can tell you. I'm sure to have a few bruises around the waist. The rope was then dropped down to Joshua and he hauled himself up, hand over hand. I was shaking even more than I usually do and could hardly speak.' She gave a weak laugh. 'I was glad they brought a stretcher because I would never have been able to walk back.'

'Phew! We've had a real scary experience, like one of those television soapies. But I have to add that you could have been killed if it wasn't for that ledge. I'm surprised you didn't break any bones.'

'You're telling me. I'm stronger than I look.' Flashing her a devilish grin and, with a twinkle in her eyes, she asked, 'Do you still want those berries? I'll take a quick walk up the koppie tomorrow to get some for you.' She burst out laughing.

Emma chuckled. 'Don't talk to me about berries or secret hideaways. I'll stick to something safe like studying the 'Trivial Pursuit' questions.'

'Amen to that.' Elizabeth agreed. Biting her lip, she added, 'But as rough as the experience has been I have to admit it has made me feel stronger and for some unknown reason, a bit more confident.'

Emma looked at her in surprise. 'I know what you mean. I feel that way too.'

The next morning Emma and Elizabeth were the center of attraction. They had to tell their story of the koppie drama to a spellbound audience.

The morning raced by and at lunch Emma found she was too excited to eat because soon her family would be arriving. It felt as if she hadn't seen them for months, instead of only one week. She was determined that no nasty word would ever again pass through her lips.

Those who were expecting visitors assembled on the long verandah to await their arrival. Emma sat with them, clenching and unclenching her hands nervously. Her eyes searched the gateway as each car drove up and parked alongside the building, constantly glancing at her watch.

'They're ten minutes late,' she whispered, a catch in her throat. Maybe they had decided not to come after all. Tears pricked the back of her eyes. Then, excitement raced through her when she saw the blue BMW turn into the driveway. She gave a deep sigh of relief when Mother and Stacey, their faces wreathed in smiles and almost hanging out of the window, waved vigorously to her. She waved back.

A few minutes later they joined her and after hugging and kissing her Mother cried, 'You're looking wonderful. There's a fresh colour in your cheeks and the old sparkle has returned to your eyes.'

'What happened to your arms and hands?' gasped Stacey.

'It's a long story,' laughed Emma. 'I'll tell you later.'

Father chuckled and gave her a wink. 'Has my little Springbok been up to mischief already?'

Emma looked at him and smiled. 'Let's go for a walk.'

Stacey clung to her arm while Father took control of the wheelchair and they made their way around the garden.

'I'd like you to meet Elizabeth,' Emma said, suddenly. 'She's been a wonderful friend to me. I must warn you she's spastic and shakes a lot and you have to listen really carefully to understand what she's saying. Her parents live in East London and can't often visit her.'

'We'd love to meet her,' chorused her parents.

'She'll be in the rumpus room watching television. Let's go inside.'

At first when Emma introduced Elizabeth to her family she was very shy but soon warmed to their kindness. Between her and Emma they laughingly related their experiences of the previous afternoon. Mother was horrified and made them promise never to leave the premises again.

'Matron has already read the riot act to us,' Emma assured her.

'Come and see the room we share,' invited Elizabeth.

The afternoon went by all too soon and after bidding her family farewell, Emma made her way to the rumpus room. Elizabeth had left them earlier to collect a magazine from the library.

On her way to the room Emma suddenly realized that she hadn't seen Ralph all day. Could he be hiding from the visitors, she wondered. But that wasn't like him. Puzzled, she shrugged as she pushed open the door and went in.

It was crowded and all eyes were glued to the television screen. A wild life film was showing. Elizabeth saw her and beckoned to her. From the expression on her friend's face Emma knew that something was amiss.

As she drew up next to Elizabeth's chair she whispered, 'Where's Ralph?'

'I've just heard,' Elizabeth replied in an undertone, 'In the early hours of the morning he had a very bad asthma attack and had to go into an oxygen tent.'

Startled, Emma gasped. 'Where is he?'

'In the sick bay.'

Without further ado Emma propelled herself out of the room and hurried down the corridor. When she arrived at the door of the sick bay she stopped. Shaking all over, she pushed the door open, her eyes searching inside like a scared rabbit.

There was a row of beds on either side of the room. A bed at the far end, covered by what appeared to be a transparent plastic tent, caught her eye. It looked kind of spooky and raised gooseflesh on her arms. Making her way to the bed she peered uneasily at the figure lying so still.

It was Ralph!

Only a feint pulse fluttered in his throat. It reminded her of the time her grandmother was dying. She had overheard the Rev. Philipson telling her father, 'She's little more than a breath on a bed.'

A sensation, almost of panic, seized her. Could Ralph be dying, she wondered? Her courage seeped away like water gurgling out of a basin after the plug had been pulled out.

Pressing her hand to her mouth she had to muffle the cry that rose to her lips.

****

CHAPTER EIGHT

Crutches!

With sinking heart, Emma sat staring at the figure lying so still on the bed. 'It's spooky,' she whispered, a tear trickling down her cheek. As she reached in her pocket for a tissue she noticed small puffs of steam coming into the tent from a pipe connected to a cylinder on a trolley nearby.

Sensing she was being watched, she glanced uneasily at Ralph and found herself looking into dark eyes that were regarding her searchingly. Flushing under his scrutiny, she twisted uncomfortably in her chair. What was he thinking as he looked at her? Had she made a fool of herself coming here?

The eyes that now seemed to be abnormally large in his expressionless face held hers and she couldn't look away. It felt as if he was looking right into her soul and she shivered. For several seconds they just stared at each other. Then rubbing his eyes with his knuckles he slowly sat up.

Trying to look nonchalant, she asked in a hushed tone, which seemed appropriate for the gloomy ward, 'Are you all right?'

He shrugged awkwardly and appeared to be a little embarrassed. Almost as though it was against his will, he smiled. 'Yes, sort of. Matron said I could leave this prison tomorrow morning.'

Suddenly Emma felt so happy she could hardly speak. It must have shown in her face for he laughed. She thought she saw a glimmer of warmth in his eyes and colour seemed to come into his cheeks. The corners of his mouth twisted into a wide grin.

In an attempt to overcome the shyness and awkwardness that came over her she burst out, 'Elizabeth and I have decided to challenge you to a game of Trivial Pursuit next Saturday afternoon.'

Ralph nodded. 'You're on!' The smile that followed warmed his face like a light and she noticed as if for the first time his even white teeth and the long black lashes that shaded his eyes. Her eyes flickered under his steady gaze and she was relieved to hear the bell ring for supper.

'I must go now, Ralph.'

'Thanks for the visit,' he called, as she hurried from the room.

During the next few days Ralph helped Emma with her reading for Tape Aids for the Blind. Progress seemed to be agonizingly slow. He taught her how to change her voice to either a low or higher octave. At first she would break into a fit of the giggles. Ralph wasn't amused for he took this work very seriously. She couldn't stop herself, but gradually she managed to control her giggles and began to enjoy reading the story with all its emphasis on the different characters. She was nervous when Ralph made her read into the microphone for the first time and shocked when he played the tape back. When she heard her voice she felt stunned and stupid. It sounded so nasal, like a total dork.

'I'm not suited for this,' she gasped.

'That's nonsense,' was his instantaneous reply, 'You need confidence and that comes with practice. It'll eventually click.'

With his help she persisted and, as her reading improved, so did her confidence and enjoyment.

There was one story that highly amused her. It was about a cheetah having an identity crisis. King Lion of the Bushveld told him he belonged to the cat family, yet his claws were like those of a dog's. 'Cats, leopards and lions can pull their claws into their paws, but you can't do that,' said the King. There were some amusing episodes in the story, but in the end he had to learn to accept himself for what he was.

She snorted. 'Sounds like a hint for me too.'

She and Elizabeth continued to memorize the quiz questions during every spare moment and at two o'clock on Saturday afternoon they gathered in the rumpus room for their challenge game of Trivial Pursuit. Both she and Elizabeth were hyped up with suppressed excitement.

By this time the whole school knew about the competition and gathered in eager anticipation. Nurse McPherson was to be Ralph's partner and she too seemed to be bubbling with elation.

Ralph set the board on a table with its coloured squares denoting the different categories of questions.

Emma and Elizabeth shared a conspiratorial look as the game began. It progressed with the scores remaining even. Suddenly Ralph burst out laughing. Shaking his head, but with his eyes sparkling with amusement, he exclaimed, 'Why, I do believe, the two of you have been studying these questions!'

'There's no law against it,' Emma said defiantly.

'No, but we'll catch you out,' Ralph warned.

'We'll see about that,' Emma retorted.

Elizabeth burst into a fit of the giggles.

Nurse McPherson laughed and shook her head. 'All's fair in love and war!' she chuckled.

Finally, they needed only one point to win. Elizabeth clutched the dice in her hands. Please let it be history, thought Emma. History was her best subject. Elizabeth threw the dice. There was complete silence as the dice rolled once, twice, and landed with number three facing up. A murmur of excitement went round the room. Emma groaned inwardly and bit her lip. Literature! The one section she and Elizabeth were weak on.

There was a hush as everyone waited for the question. A few younger girls began giggling nervously as Ralph took out a card. He raised his eyebrows as if to say, 'I've got you now.'

'What was the family name of the three sisters who each had a book published?' Ralph asked.

Emma hadn't a clue and she looked desperately at Elizabeth, who was frowning. Sighing, Emma steeled herself for failure.

Elizabeth nudged her and she was surprised to see she was smiling. 'It's from my group,' she tried to whisper to Emma. 'I know the answer.' Turning to Ralph she replied, 'The Bronte sisters.'

'Correct!' exclaimed Ralph, in astonishment and disbelief. 'Congratulations! You've won,' he said, shaking his head, a ghost of a smile hovering about his lips.

A shout went up from the onlookers.

Emma felt a sudden warm rush of pleasure.

Elizabeth hugged her. 'We're now the reigning champions,' she cried, gleefully. 'What do you say about that, Mr. Ralph Masters?'

Ralph just grinned.

Nurse McPherson smiled. 'Congratulations,' she said and winked at them. Turning to Ralph she added, 'Challenge them to another game. Luck also plays a part in this. Who knows, we may beat them next time.'

His face lit up. 'Right! You did very well, even if you did study the questions. How about another game soon?'

'Fine by us.' Emma replied.

On the following Monday afternoon Emma looked all over for Ralph. He wasn't in his room and no one had seen him since lunch. A feeling of concern came over her. Could it be that he was back in the sick bay, she wondered. She was about to go and look when she heard a voice beside her.

It was Nurse McPherson. 'Hello Emma, looking for Ralph?'

'Yes,' she replied.

Nurse McPherson laughed. 'On Saturday morning Dr Stephenson sent him next door to the laboratory to take a blood sample for analysis. Now he wants to spend every available moment of his time there.'

Emma gave a sigh of relief.

Nurse McPherson chuckled. 'Dr Mostert, the Pathologist, is most impressed with our Ralph and says he has the makings of a very good Medical Technologist.' She smiled. 'He'll be back soon, Emma,' she added as she walked away.

Emma felt hurt. Why didn't he say something to her? She thought they were good friends. The readings for Tape Aids for the Blind were now completed for the time being and Ralph had suggested she learn how to play chess, but she hadn't been too keen. She gritted her teeth. 'If that's the way he wants it see if I care,' she hissed.

At supper she picked him out about not telling her where he had spent the afternoon.

He looked at her blankly. 'Give me a break! You're not my mother! Why should I have to tell you?'

Taken aback, and with a tilt of her chin, she snapped, 'Common curtsey.' She wanted to add that she thought they had an understanding. Instead, she kept quiet. An awkward silence fell between them.

She glared at him and he glowered back at her.

Then he hissed, 'Buzz off! I'm my own person,' and wheeled away.

'You really are a prat!' she called after him. 'An unpredictable prat!'

For the next few days they avoided each other. Elizabeth was curious, but didn't say anything and Emma didn't want to talk about it.

The following day, Mrs Hart, the therapist, told Emma she was to be fitted for calipers. Emma could hardly believe what she was hearing and felt elated and apprehensive all at once.

'I think you'll be able to cope with them,' Mrs Hart said. 'It should take a week or ten days to be made up. Once they're fitted you'll be shown how to walk, with the assistance of crutches, of course.'

A wave of fresh hope passed over Emma. Once the calipers were fitted maybe the time would come when she could walk without crutches like some of the other children. As the optimism welled up within her the years ahead glowed more and more with the hope that an almost normal life still awaited her. She was so excited she wanted to rush out to the koppie and shout it to the hill tops. She giggled. 'Matron would have something to say about that.'

The next morning before school, to her surprise, Ralph came up to her. 'I hear you'll be joining the 'Caliper Brigade'.

'Good news travels fast in this place,' she replied warily. Then, throwing caution to the wind, she burst out, 'Oh, Ralph, I want to walk more than anything else in the whole world.'

'Wouldn't that be great,' he said, simply, with obvious warmth. 'No such luck for me, ever.' For a moment an odd haunted look came into his eyes.

'Ralph,' Emma began and then realized that Ralph would forever be wheelchair bound and this no doubt could sadden him. She was about to ask him why he had been so angry with her, but changed her mind. Put it down to another of his doom and gloom periods.

'Yes?' urged Ralph.

'Oh, nothing,' she said offhandedly.

Each night before dropping off to sleep she pictured walking to school with the calipers concealed under her jeans. Cripples used crutches. She would no longer be a cripple because she was convinced that the time would come when the calipers would be all she needed. Her walk may be different, but who cares about that. Returning to her old school could be a possibility, and a normal life.

Ralph seemed to seek her out and in little ways tried to show her how sorry he was for the way he had been treating her. Emma was still wary of him though she enjoyed hearing about the work in the laboratory. She wished she could go with him even for an afternoon, yet she was loathed to mention it.

When her family visited her she spoke about the calipers, but didn't reveal her secret hope that she wouldn't require crutches for long. They were as excited as she was. 'You'll be able to come home for the holidays soon,' Stacey said, excitedly.

Emma's eyes lit up. 'Yes, yes, and yes,' she cried.

Emma chose the opportunity to introduce Ralph to her family. They took to him immediately and she could see he was pleased.

The following week Emma's calipers were ready. They extended from her feet to almost half way up her thighs. Mrs. Hart eased her feet into the surgical shoes that were fitted to the irons.

Emma caught her breath as Mrs Hart helped her to her feet and led her to the parallel bars. How strange it was for her to be able to stand again. Suddenly she was absolutely terrified.

'Hold on to the bars,' encouraged Mrs Hart, 'and try to swing both legs forward and see how far you can go along the bars. You've got good strong arm muscles and should manage fine.'

After several attempts Emma found she could swing her legs by moving her lower body forward.

Mrs. Hart was pleased. 'Good! You've done well. Keep it up. In a day or so we'll try out the crutches.'

With her well-developed shoulder and arm muscles, Emma experienced no difficulty in using the crutches and could walk with comparative ease. She continued to exercise daily on the parallel bars. As her ability to move along them increased, so her confidence grew.

After about three weeks her dexterity had grown to such an extent that Emma felt sure she would be able to walk without the aid of crutches and so, one afternoon, she slipped into the therapy room. With her hands on the parallel bars she allowed the crutches to fall to the floor and found herself joining them. Pulling herself up painfully she tried again to move one leg forward and then the other, but with the same result. Again and again she tried and kept losing her balance. The awful truth came to her that she would never be able to maintain her balance without the aid of crutches.

Finally, she clung to the bars. 'I'll never walk without these darn crutches,' she sobbed, dropping to the floor with a thunk, lying in an ungainly heap.

Ralph wheeled in through the door. He stopped when he saw her on the floor with her face buried in her hands. 'Emma!' he called softly.

Humiliated, she shouted, 'Get out of here and leave me alone!'

He shook his head in bewilderment and left.

****

CHAPTER NINE

The Laboratory

Emma felt a rage growing within her as all the old bitterness and resentment returned. She pulled herself up wearily, placed the crutches under her arms, and made her way slowly back to the room.

The corridor was empty and she realized that the bell must have rung for tea. Even though there was a mouth-watering smell of savoury tart drifting towards her, she said huffily, 'I don't want any.'

When she reached the room she discarded the crutches, sat on the bed and pulled first her one leg up and then the other, resting her head on the pillows. The stillness in the room was heavy. She felt as if her blood had all drained out leaving her limp. If only she could see into the future, just a tiny bit of it. 'Will I ever be able to walk without crutches?' she demanded, beating her fists furiously on the bed. A heavy weight seemed to press down on her.

About ten minutes later Elizabeth walked in. 'Where have you been?' she cried, looking anxiously at Emma.

'I didn't want any tea,' Emma snapped.

'I was worried about you. That bruise on your arm!' A note of alarm came into Elizabeth's voice and she rushed to her.

'Please leave me alone,' Emma gulped, her eyes smarting with tears.

Elizabeth sat at the bottom of Emma's bed and shook her head in despair. 'Tell me what happened.'

Emma glanced defiantly at her. 'I tried to walk.' She burst into tears and then added between sobs, 'But I couldn't without crutches. I was so convinced that once the calipers were fitted to my legs I would soon be able to walk. But it hasn't happened. I don't want to have to use crutches. I want to be like the other kids who manage to walk only with the aid of calipers.' She paused and drew in her breath. 'Using crutches makes me a cripple.'

Elizabeth reached across and took Emma's hands in hers. 'But Emma, don't delude yourself. You ARE a cripple whether you use crutches or not. Can't you just be glad you're out of the wheelchair, at least for now?' Biting her lip, she added, her eyes softening, 'You were far happier then.'

Emma wrenched her hands free and briefly covered her face. 'I know, that was before I knew there was an escape from the wheelchair. Now I know better. I'm never giving up. I'm going to keep on trying to walk without crutches. Haven't you heard of 'If at first you don't succeed and all that jazz?'

Elizabeth was momentarily speechless. Then she took her hands once more. 'Wake up! Welcome to the real world. Don't you see,' she said quietly, 'that you'll keep hurting yourself. You're a stubborn and determined type of person which is good, but there are some things you won't be able to change no matter how hard you try, try and try again, and you'll have to learn to accept it like so many others have had to do.'

Emma felt her face flush and she shook her head angrily. 'It's all very well for you to talk!' she exclaimed, feeling a momentary twinge of pity when she saw the pain in Elizabeth's face, but she was too angry to care. 'You can walk!'

Elizabeth's mouth had dropped open in surprise and she gulped once or twice before saying softly, 'You 're so very wrong. I can walk, yes, but look at me. I'm constantly shaking and speak as if I have a marshmallow or two in my mouth. Who'd you rather be?' Her voice dropped to a whisper. 'Most people think spastics are feeble-minded. Whenever I went home and saw my lovely sister, Carol, living a normal life I tried hard to shake off the envy and resentment that built up inside me. When I met Carol's very fashionable friends for the first time they stared uncomfortably at me and I felt like a pariah. I'm what you could call 'fashion challenged'. Fashion has never been a priority for me, not that the latest fashions would make any difference to my skinny figure.' She laughed.

Emma sat upright on the bed. Suddenly she felt very small and ashamed. 'Don't talk like that, Elizabeth.'

Elizabeth ignored her. 'They pretended I wasn't there and asked others questions about me like, 'Do you think she'd like an orange juice'. You'd think I was a freak in a sideshow. I made up my mind that I'd rather stay here where I felt safe and hidden from the world.' She sighed again. 'It hurts and it makes me angry when I meet people for the first time and they only see my disability. I'm not completely useless. I've never told anyone this before, but sometimes I used to wake up in the early hours of the morning feeling depressed, not knowing how I would cope with the day ahead. It's such an empty, alone feeling. I'm sure others here will know exactly what I mean.'

An awkward silence fell over them. Elizabeth stared directly at Emma with large unfocused eyes while she slipped back into the past. 'A while ago, before you arrived, Ralph and I were talking about the same thing and he told me he too went through times when he became very depressed. He would worry about tomorrow and nurse resentment, frightened at having his whole life ahead of him and not a clue about what he could do.'

Elizabeth smiled wanly. 'Everyone has their own secret battle to fight. You've seen Ralph's legs.'

Emma nodded.

'He told me there were two reasons why he kept them covered. One, so that people couldn't see them.'

Emma whispered, 'And the other?'

'So that he wouldn't have to see them. I don't know what happened, but although he still keeps his legs covered he's obviously developed a more carefree attitude towards life in general. Don't you agree?'

'I do,' Emma put in, 'more than anyone I've ever met. He packs so much into every waking hour I sometimes feel tired just watching him.'

Elizabeth laughed. 'He once told me that no one's going to open doors for you if you don't knock.' Her eyes sparkled. 'Oh, Emma, I don't want us to fight each other. You're the best thing that's happened to me, the first real friend I've ever had. As someone once said, 'The world is a lovelier place because you are in it.'

Emma stared incredulously at her. 'Elizabeth!' she spluttered, 'You're my best friend too.' Nothing in the world meant more to her at that moment. She hadn't realized how much Elizabeth had valued their friendship and it touched her deeply.

'Thanks, Emma,' Elizabeth came back. 'I needed to hear that. Hopefully I'll pass my matriculation this year.'

'No fear about that,' Emma scoffed. 'What am I going to do when you leave?'

Elizabeth smiled reassuringly. 'Someone else will take my place.'

'Perish the thought,' Emma muttered.

'I'm so looking forward to entering the computer world.'

Emma nodded. 'I know, and I'm happy for you.'

A light came into Elizabeth's eyes as she continued, 'A few months before you arrived, I was worried about my future. I didn't want to be a burden to anyone, especially my family. I was in the library one day when I found a book called, 'The Beast of Business'. It was all about computers. A lot dealt with the problems that arose if incorrect information and instructions are fed into a computer. It pointed out that if computers are correctly used they could do wonderful things. They are also merciless, moronic and unthinking.' She laughed. 'There were some peculiar expressions in the book such as 'GIGO', Garbage In and Garbage Out, which means if 'garbage' is put into a computer only 'garbage' will come out of it. My interest was aroused and I read several other books, especially ordered for me from the Town Library.'

'I've tried reading some of the computer books and it's all Greek to me,' Emma broke in. 'There's so much jargon I don't understand.'

'You'll soon learn,' Elizabeth said emphatically. 'Matron saw me reading one of the books and the result was a computer company invited me to do an aptitude test and I came up with an over ninety per cent pass.'

Emma was impressed. 'Goodness gracious me!' she gasped. 'Ralph wasn't fooling when he said you were good, no not good, brilliant.'

Elizabeth giggled. 'Don't get carried away now, Emma. It's just my luck I've discovered that I have a computer brain more than one for history or literature. To make a long story shorter the computer company has offered me a position when I get my matriculation.'

'So your future's assured,' was Emma's instantaneous reply, 'that's more than I can say for mine.'

Elizabeth looked at her intently. 'You've still got plenty of time to find out what you want to do. Until computers came into my life I pictured myself as some sort of clerk in an office hidden in a corner so that people would not be gaping at me. But now, I feel as good as anyone else. It's a wonderful feeling knowing I no longer see myself as digging a hole somewhere and crawling into it so that no one will notice me. My outlook has changed completely. I'm even confident enough to take on my sister's fashionable friends.'

Her white teeth flashed into a grin. 'As you know I'm what you call coloured. Coloured is such a stupid word. It could mean green, pink or blue, but you know what I mean?'

Emma smiled and nodded.

'My great, great grandfather on my mother's side was a Xhosa. He worked at a mission station in the Transkei and married the white missionary's daughter. They had seven children, four girls and three boys. Two of the girls took after his wife and they were classified as white and lost touch with the family.'

'How sad,' Emma chimed in. 'Hasn't anyone tried to trace that part of the family?'

'No,' Elizabeth said offhandedly. 'Just think, Emma, what happened all those years ago affects future generations. I am what I am because of what my great, great grandfather did so many years ago. If he had married a Xhosa woman I would have been someone else.' She sighed and added sadly, 'Maybe a normal person. But I mustn't whinge against fate. I am what I am and that can't be changed. My mother did tell me that there were problems with my birth and the damage was caused then.'

Emma shivered. 'You wouldn't have been you and I couldn't bear that.'

Elizabeth was silent for a moment. 'What would I have been? I'm part of my mother and father. That means my mother and even her mother would have been different people.' She threw up her hands in despair. 'It's too much for a mere mortal like me to understand.'

'And me too,' Emma put in, screwing up her face in distaste. 'It works for everyone. If my father had married another person instead of my mother, I too would have been someone else, maybe someone who didn't like sport.' She bit her lip thoughtfully. 'Is everything preordained by forces over which we have no control?'

Elizabeth burst out laughing. 'Who would know! Please, this is getting too much,' she begged. 'Let's stop. I've really started something crazy.'

Emma gave her a soft smile. 'It's what my father would call trivia. He says we all have a store of it in our minds and it's fun to bring out every now and again to give us a good laugh. And to stop us from taking ourselves too seriously.'

During the next few days Emma avoided Ralph. She couldn't face him after her outburst in the therapy room. Each afternoon she still continued to try to walk without crutches often falling and bruising badly. Once she hit her forehead on the end of one of the bars and almost knocked herself out. Angrily she grabbed her crutches and left the room.

In the corridor she almost bumped into Ralph. He stared at her for a moment or two, opened his mouth to speak, decided against it, and hurried away.

Hurt and humiliated, Emma went to her room. 'He can get lost!' she spat out. An onrush of hatred came over her such as she'd never known before and she was startled by its fierceness. 'What's happening to me? I'm going back to my old bitter days. It's got to stop and now!'

When Elizabeth saw the large shiny bump on her forehead she cried out in despair. 'Emma, when are you going to learn?'

'I'll never give up!' she said venomously. 'But I won't be crabby again.' She laughed and added, 'I promise.'

Elizabeth snorted. 'I'll hold you to it.'

But Emma found it impossible. No matter how hard she tried she couldn't walk without crutches. Her rage almost took control of her. Then she sighed. 'Maybe Elizabeth's right. I'll never be able to walk without crutches. I suppose I should be glad I'm out of the wheelchair. Father's always on about accepting the things you cannot change. I'll forget about it for a while.' Grinning with something like her old sparkle, she went to find Elizabeth.

The next morning at school Emma caught Ralph staring at her, a hurt and puzzled expression on his face. She felt a compulsion to go over and talk to him, but couldn't. Instead, she quickly looked away and carried on with her work. She had regretted, over and over again, her outburst in the therapy room in front of him and felt a total idiot.

After school Ralph waylaid her in the corridor. 'Why are you angry with me, Emma?' he asked.

'Are you the only one allowed to go through dark and gloomy periods?' she asked haughtily.

He replied awkwardly, 'I suppose I rather asked for that. I'm sorry.' His face brightened. 'We never did have that wheelchair race.'

'Now we never will,' she retorted, 'much to Matron's relief I'm sure.'

There was a long silence because no one could think of what to say. Ralph was about to turn away when Emma said sheepishly, 'I made a twit of myself the other afternoon, didn't I?'

For a moment he didn't respond. Then his face relaxed and he smiled, small wrinkles fanning out from the corners of his eyes. The warmth of his smile made her feel 'as secure as a baby wrapped in a fluffy angora blanket' she thought and grinned. 'Let's forget it,' he said. 'Nurse Mcpherson's on duty this weekend and available for a rematch of Trivial Pursuit. How about it?'

An amused glint came into Emma's eyes. 'Maybe. I'll speak to Elizabeth and let you know.'

'OK, it's up to you.'

He looked so woebegone that Emma couldn't resist reaching out and gently touching his arm. Realizing what she had done she pulled her hand away, blushing profusely. 'What got into me,' she moaned.

Ralph, his eyes sparkling, threw back his head and roared with laughter, wheeling himself down the corridor and into his room.

The following day he once again waylaid her in the corridor after school. 'Would you like to come with me to the laboratory this afternoon?' I've asked permission from Dr Mostert, the Pathologist, and he has agreed.

Emma's face lit up. 'Oh, Ralph, I'd love to come.'

'I can show you some easy tests.' He paused. 'But it'll be better for you to use your wheelchair.'

Emma stared at him aghast! Go back into her wheelchair! He must have flipped his lid! Definitely there's no way I'm going back to that!

Ralph must have read her thoughts. 'Only for convenience, Emma,' he explained, 'even the physically normal people have to sit. Dr Mostert and the others in the lab have chairs on wheels. They have to move from one test to another and Dr Mostert once told me it was too exhausting and hard on the legs to be jumping up and down all day long. The wheel chairs they use are not for the likes of us. There's not enough support in them.'

'All right,' she agreed, reluctantly.

Later, as Ralph led the way into the laboratory, a tall wiry built man with receding fair hair and warm dark blue eyes, who reminded Emma of her father, looked up from a microscope he had been peering into and hastened over to them, his face wreathed in smiles.

'Hello, Ralph, my son,' he greeted.

'Dr Mostert,' Ralph began, 'I would like to introduce you to my friend, Emma du Preez.'

Emma shook hands and smiled shyly at him.

After being introduced to the other assistants, Ralph said, 'Come, Emma, let me show you around.'

Dr Mostert nodded approvingly and returned to his microscope.

Although Emma was at first overawed by all the complex equipment, she soon found herself fascinated by what she saw and when an hour later Ralph told her it was time for them to leave, she was loathe to go.

On their way back, a few meters from the entrance to Happiness Inn, Ralph stopped and pointed to a line of hills low on the horizon.

'I recognize the little koppie on the right,' Emma told him. 'I'm sure that's where Elizabeth and I had our adventure.'

Ralph nodded. 'Could be. Those hills, whenever I look at them they are always a different colour.'

The lower slopes were shrouded in mist and the outline of their peaks was softly blended into the late afternoon sky.

'I often wonder what lies on the other side of them,' he mumbled, as if to himself. 'They always look so mysterious.'

'From that little koppie we could see a beautiful valley and misty mountains that stretched for many kilometers,' Emma told him.

He laughed. 'Come, let's go.'

She followed and just before they were about to go into the building, Ralph stopped. Like a whirlwind he grabbed her chair and twirled it around so that she was close beside him. He reached out and grabbed her by both wrists, bending his head towards hers. Her eyes rested on his lips. Then his mouth touched hers and her whole being lit up with an incredible sweetness. The next minute he was racing into the building anxious to get away as quickly as possible.

Emma, completely taken by surprise, tenderly touched her lips. Then her face changed to a look of joy and she whispered, 'I love you too, Ralph Masters.'

Turning her wheelchair around, she made her way into the building.

Nurse McPherson was standing at the door, a sad look on her face. There were tears trembling on her eyelashes. Quickly she turned and hurried away.

Strange, Emma thought, she must have had some bad news. She looked around for Ralph, but he was nowhere to be seen. Chuckling, she made her way to her room, her mind in a whirl. There was a warm pink glow on her cheeks. Ralph loved her and that made her feel special.

****

CHAPTER TEN

The Diary

Before supper that evening Emma was surprised to hear that Ralph had another asthma attack. Matron had quickly bundled him off to the sick bay and into the oxygen tent.

She pondered about the reason for this latest attack because he now had two in a short space of time. Could the strain of showing her all the tests at the laboratory have been too much for him? Surely not, he used more energy tearing up and down the corridor at break neck speed.

She called to see him and he gave her a sheepish grin. Memories of the kiss made her blush and she dropped her eyes to stare at the floor. Then, looking up she asked, 'How...how are you feeling?' Her voice faltered under his steady gaze and her heart beat so hard she was sure he could hear it.

'Fine, just fine,' he assured her, with a wave of his hand. 'I've been brought here as a precaution. Matron said I'll be back in my room a little later.'

The last of the sun's rays shone through the window illuminating the room with a golden glow. A smile lit up her face. 'I'm so glad,' she whispered, adding, 'I can't stay now. The bell's already gone for supper. If you don't mind, I'll call and see you later, say about seven.'

His eyes were shining as he replied enthusiastically, 'Good. I'd like that.'

She felt a frisson of electricity go through her as she hurried away. Sniggering, she murmured, 'It would have made my toes curl if I could feel them.'

When Emma went to Ralph's room that evening he was sleeping peacefully. She stole quietly away.

The next morning she learned that Ralph had a slight cold and had been confined to bed.

Before school she hurried to his room to find out how he was. On receiving no response to her tap on the door she pushed it open uncertainly and went inside. She stared speechlessly at Ralph lying on his back propped up with pillows, frantically using an asthmatic spray and breathing heavily in gasps and wheezes.

He looked so desperately tired and small, like a very young child. She had never seen anyone having an asthma attack, and for a moment just gaped at him wide-eyed. 'Hello, Ralph,' she called softly.

He stared at her with large unfocused eyes. As recognition came to him he turned his head away. 'I wish you hadn't come,' he said, gruffly, his voice strained and with a hint of reproof. 'I don't like you seeing me like this. Please leave. I'll be fine in a few minutes.'

Emma was about to reply, but a fit of coughing racked his thin frame. Some sixth sense warned her that he needed help in a hurry.

Panic-stricken, she told him, 'I'm going to find Nurse McPherson or Matron,' and hurried from the room.

Matron was walking towards her along the corridor.

'Matron!' she called, 'Ralph…'

Before she could continue, Matron, her face grave, replied, 'All right, my dear, I'll see to Ralph. He'll be fine in a short while. You go to school.' She hurried into the room.

After school Emma went to Ralph's room. He wasn't there. A feeling of dread came over her and she hurried to the sick bay, giving a long sigh of relief when she saw him sitting up in bed reading a magazine. She was relieved to see the strained look had gone. He gazed at her for a long moment, his eyes questioning, then he grinned as if he knew exactly how she felt. Her cheeks warmed. 'It's impossible to keep a good man down for long,' he said, his dark eyes sparkling with amusement.

She had to admit he looked terrific. He wasn't good-looking, but his smile and sparkling eyes made up for the lack of good looks.

She moistened her lips with the tip of her tongue. 'You really gave me such a fright this morning,' she told him. Realizing that her words may have sounded like a reprimand, she added, 'I'm glad you are better.'

'I'll be back in my room a little later. I'm afraid we won't be able to go to the laboratory this afternoon, but we'll go tomorrow.'

'Sure. What can I do for you?'

'Nothing, really,' he came back. Then he surprised her by adding shyly; 'will you come and see me again?'

'Of course, I will,' she promised.

He smiled back as if she had paid him the biggest compliment.

They looked into each other's eyes for what seemed like a long time. Then he took her hand in his and her fingers tingled at his touch.

The bell rang for lunch. 'I'd better go.' She removed her hand, turned and hurried away.

When she reached the door Ralph called, 'Hey!'

She turned. 'Yes?'

'You're so good with those crutches I'm sure you could race me in my wheelchair.'

She threw up her eyes to heaven piously and then giggled. 'Can you just imagine that? You can think up some ridiculous things at times, Ralph Masters.'

She heard him laughing as she made her way to the dining room.

After lunch she eagerly went to Ralph's room. He was waiting for her shuffling a pack of cards. Resting her crutches against the bed, she made herself comfortable in a chair beside him. During the next hour or so he showed her how to play the game of 'patience' and a few card tricks.

Shaking her head in amazement she asked, 'Where could you possibly have learned all these things?'

His lips lifted in the corners in a ghost of a smile. 'Now that would be telling.' He laughed. 'But I'll be kind to you and give my secrets away.'

She sniggered. 'What have I done to deserve this great honour?'

'It's so simple,' he informed. 'From the library, from books. We have a wonderful library here and Miss Lategan will order anything you need from the main branch in town. I must warn you the card tricks take a lot of practice.'

'Mmmh, like most things,' Emma said thoughtfully. 'I've never been great on reading. In the past most of my time was spent at the gym. I'll certainly explore the library in future. Elizabeth spends a great deal of time devouring computer books there, but I have noticed an occasional love story lying on her bedside table.'

Ralph laughed. 'Love stories I can't comment on, but all that reading on computers has paid off for her.'

The afternoon seemed to fly past and now and again their hands touched and once he held her hand tightly and it looked as though he was about to say something. Instead, he grinned, his dark eyes bright with amusement, and released her hand. She felt sorry when the time came to leave and wished he would kiss her again, blushing at the thought.

'I'll see you at school tomorrow,' he said as she walked away.

Sometime during that night Emma woke briefly. Through the mist of sleep she seemed to hear a noise as if someone or something was being wheeled quickly down the corridor. Turning on to her stomach she went back to sleep.

Dawn had scarcely broken when she awoke with a start, eyes flicking wide, staring. She sat up sharply as if electrocuted when she remembered the vague sounds she had heard during the night. Immediately the blood rushed to her face and a sense of panic threatened to overwhelm her. Instinct told her that something was wrong and a feeling of doom sank into her stomach. She gave a sudden shocked gasp.

Ralph!

But it couldn't be. He was so well after his last asthma attack.

Looking across at Elizabeth she saw that she was still sleeping soundly. Quickly putting on her calipers that stood next to the bed and, after slipping on her dressing gown, she put the crutches under her arms and made her way out of the room.

No one was about.

She hurried to Ralph's room and tapped softly on the door.

There was no reply.

She tapped again. Then, pushing the door open she peered inside. The curtains were closed. In the half-light she could make out Ralph's roommates, Jackson and Ted, still asleep, but Ralph's bed was empty!

She was filled with a strange foreboding and had an eerie feeling she was never going to hear his voice again. It made her whole body shudder. Somewhere far off an owl hooted. Stiffening, she hurried down the corridor to the sick bay. As she drew near a nurse came out.

'What are you doing up at this hour?' she asked, surprised.

Before Emma could reply Nurse McPherson rushed out. 'Call Matron,' she told the nurse.

The nurse hurried off down the corridor.

A cold hand seemed to grip at Emma's heart. Now she knew the meaning of the saying 'and my blood ran cold'. The look on Nurse McPherson's face said more than any words could tell and Emma's heart began beating wildly, her eyes wide. 'Is Ralph,' she began. She didn't want to hear any bad news, but couldn't bear not to know.

Nurse McPherson looked pityingly at her. 'Ralph passed away a few minutes ago, Emma. His chest was too weak. He had another bad asthma attack and his heart just gave in.' Her voice faded.

Emma gave a low stifled moan and jerked forward almost falling to the ground. Nurse McPherson put her arms around her to steady her. Emma stared over the nurse's shoulder at the door of the sick bay. Invisible cold fingers gripped her heart and she had to stifle the scream that rose up in her throat.

Almost not daring to, she asked, 'Is he still in there?' The thought of Ralph's body lying on the bed was horrifying. A sharp pain seemed trapped inside her as though in an invisible cage not able to escape.

Nurse Mcpherson nodded. 'He's at peace now.'

Emma's lips quivered. 'Could it be that he's only sleeping?'

Nurse McPherson looked steadily at Emma. 'No, my child.'

'Are you very sure?' Emma gasped, in disbelief. Never before had she experienced a death of someone so young and she felt confused. When her grandmother had died she was still very young and Grandmother was very old. Grandfather had died before she was born. And then there was their neighbour's husband across the road. He had a sudden heart attack and died. But she didn't like him and was almost pleased she wouldn't have to see him again.

Nurse McPherson's voice broke into her thoughts. 'Yes, Emma, I am sure Ralph's gone. Dr. Stephenson's in the sick bay with him.' She tried to smile. 'Come, I'll take you back to your room.'

Emma walked with the nurse along the corridor her eyes burning with unshed tears. She couldn't cry even if she wanted to. The sadness went too deep. It was as though she was moving through a terrible dream, so terrible it couldn't possibly be real.

Nurse Mcpherson left her at the door and hurried on down the corridor.

Elizabeth was awake when she walked into the room. 'What's happened?' she queried, looking at Emma's stricken face. 'Where have you been? I first thought you had an urgent call of nature, but when I checked no one was there. Is there a problem with your family? You look terrible.'

Emma stared blankly at her for a moment or so before blurting out, 'Ralph's dead!'

Elizabeth opened and closed her mouth several times before finding her voice. 'When? How?' she began and couldn't go on.

Something inside of Emma seemed to snap and she fell on to the bed, bursting into tears.

Elizabeth jumped from the bed and rushed to her, cradling her head in her arms. 'Oh, Emma, I'm so sorry.'

The whole school was bathed in gloom and Emma spent the morning in a turmoil of doubt and despair trying to fight back the burning lump in her throat and the dull pain deep inside her that wouldn't go away. She felt empty in a way she couldn't explain and found it hard to concentrate on her work. It was a relief when the bell finally rang to end school. After lunch she went to her room and lay on the bed. Elizabeth was attending another computer programming course. Emma wanted to cry out with rage against all the unhappiness she felt. Just when things were coming right in her life, up comes this tragedy from out of nowhere. Picking up a book from the bedside table she began to read, but the words just swam before her eyes.

There were footsteps in the corridor and Emma was surprised when Nurse McPherson came in. She was carrying a book and a small writing pad. Placing the book on the bedside table she sat at the bottom of the bed. Her eyes were underlined with tiredness.

'When you get a chance, Emma, will you take the book back to Dr Mostert at the laboratory? It has his name inside. I found it amongst Ralph's belongings.'

'Yes, Nurse, I'll do that,' she promised, looking at her curiously.

Nurse McPherson handed the writing pad to Emma. 'This is a diary of sorts written by Ralph,' she said. 'He was such a considerate young man, unusual for someone so young. The two of you became very good friends, didn't you?'

Under her scrutiny Emma made a visible effort to calm herself. 'Yyyes,' she stammered.

'I'm sorry, my dear, but if it's any consolation he also valued your friendship. He once told me how much he admired your courage and determination.'

A churning feeling started in Emma's stomach. It always did that when she was scared, and at that moment she was petrified. Ralph's diary was in her hands!

'I'd like you to read it. The diary may help you to bear your grief more easily. When you've finished reading it I must send it to some of his family members together with all his other belongings.' She sighed deeply. 'We're all going to miss not seeing Ralph around the place. He was such a likable person. Oh, he had his difficult moments but then who's perfect?' She tried to smile but it turned into a grimace. 'You will see from the diary that Ralph knew there was a strong possibility that he may die of asthma, one of those unexplained feelings that you can never fully understand. He began having the attacks a few years ago. Sometimes he could ward them off with a mouth spray he carried with him, but they gradually grew worse. One day he spoke to me about them after one of his stints in the oxygen tent.'

Without realizing what she was doing Emma sat up and rested her head against the back of the bed. The nurse took Emma's hands in hers and Emma could feel the anguish in her as she sat recalling the conversation with Ralph.

She inhaled several times. 'He asked if he only had a short time to live. I tried to shrug off the question and told him he was too young to talk about dying, but he wasn't convinced.'

'He knew he was going to die!' Emma whispered. 'And he never said a word to anyone.'

'Yes. His chest was very weak. He was born with underdeveloped lungs and his illness also had an affect on them. He knew his chances of getting better were slight. I didn't tell him this, he guessed. After our talk he became very quiet and thoughtful. I could feel his sadness. It worried me because I didn't know how to comfort him.'

Nurse McPherson's face relaxed into a smile. 'When I visited him later he was bubbling with enthusiasm. I couldn't believe the sudden change. He told me he had decided that life is not about lying down and giving up to self pity. He set himself a goal promising himself that he would matriculate and then qualify as a medical technologist. I can't remember how I replied, but I did as much as I could to encourage him. Sometimes we underestimate people's courage.' She bit her lip and looked hard at Emma. 'I witnessed Ralph kissing you that day and felt so sad and angry that fate could be so harsh.'

Emma gasped. She remembered that moment when she had seen tears in the nurse's eyes. Never in a million years would she have associated it with her and Ralph at that time.

Glancing at her watch, Nurse McPherson exclaimed, 'Good gracious!' she exclaimed, 'I must hurry. Bye for now.'

'Goodbye, Nurse, and thank you,' Emma responded. It was the longest conversation they had ever had.

She looked at Ralph's diary in her hands and whispered, 'Ralph's dead!' The word 'dead' sounded so horrible, so final, which it was, of course. It was hard to imagine Ralph dead when she had spoken to him only yesterday. She closed her eyes and moaned softly at the agony she felt deep inside. 'No one can prepare you for something like this,' she murmured.

She looked at the writing on the pad, Ralph's writing. In bold capitals were the words, ***'THE DIARY OF RALPH MASTERS.'*** A strange sensation of unreality sent a shiver down her spine. Mother once said after a burglary at their home, 'It's bad enough having our TV and video stolen, it's also an invasion of our privacy coming into our home.' Would she be invading Ralph's privacy if she read his diary? But Nurse McPherson had given it to her to read.

She clicked her tongue angrily. In normal circumstances, yes, she chided. But he's dead, she reasoned, shuddering.

Tentatively, she lifted the cover and began to read:

'For some unknown reason I have the sudden urge to write my autobiography. It's usual to start at the beginning of one's life, but that part of me is like a blur

in my mind. I have so little knowledge of my early years.

Maybe as my writing progresses my subconscious will begin to release some of my early memories and I'll be able to flash back into that period of my life. These writings will be more like sketches of events until I can get into some kind of order.

I lived with my grandmother in a rural village in a remote part of Mpumalunga. I remember Grandmother telling me that when I was born the midwife told my mother that I was stillborn. Then to everyone's amazement ten minutes later I suddenly began to cry. Many times since my illness I wished that I had died at birth. Why live only to become an asthmatic and a cripple? It was all so futile.'

Emma shivered and looked around the room aware of a presence that seemed to suddenly enter it. Could it be Ralph, she wondered, coming to comfort me? It's the type of thing he would do. Then she bit her lip thoughtfully. 'Or did he want me to stop reading his private thoughts?'

Cold, invisible fingers gripped at her and she quickly closed the pad.

****

CHAPTER ELEVEN

A magic castle

Emma's eyes burned with unshed tears. 'Grief is intolerable and cruel,' she sniffed. She hurt as she had never hurt before. Then she smiled as an image of Ralph popped into her mind. There was a mischievous twinkle in his eyes. Somehow she knew he would want her to read his diary.

Slowly, she opened up the pad and continued to read:

'Trying to visualize what Grandmother looked like is getting more and more difficult. I remember she was small and timid like a mouse and always seemed to be apologizing for something or other. I'm sure she would apologize for breathing the same air as everyone else if asked to do so. Her hair was pure white and matted like a rug close to her scalp.

I wondered if Grandfather could have beaten Grandmother because often when he was around I would find her crying and huddled in a corner of the hut. Grandfather only came home for an occasional weekend (fortunately). But his weekends started from Friday until Tuesday morning. That was a loooong time! When he was there, life was tense. I'm glad he didn't live with us full time. Life would have been unbearable. His eyes were dark and cold like ice, enough to scare the living daylights out of anyone. He ignored me completely and regularly shouted at Grandmother to get rid of that bastard. I knew he meant me and I would hide away in fear.

Grandfather and the other men spent the nights sitting around the fire outside the huts telling stories and drinking skokiaan, spending most of the day sleeping.

I often spent time with Mama Rosa, the woman who lived next door. She was much younger than Grandmother and would take me with her when she visited her daughter's khaya in the next village. She had a son, Tokyo, who was my age. He and I played together. I felt good being there.

Mama Rosa would tell us stories of her childhood and stories her father told her. These stories were repeated over and over again, but I never grew tired of hearing them. When story time was over, Tokyo and me played leapfrog and marbles. Those were happy times and I desperately wished I could have stayed there forever.

Tokyo was full of fun and daring, far more daring than I was. I wasn't daring at all. He caught field mice and lizards with his bare hands and once a mouse bit his finger so hard it was difficult to stop the bleeding. Mama Rosa was very angry, the only time I ever saw her angry. 'You're not to pick up mice or rats,' she scolded. 'They are dirty creatures and bring bad sickness.'

The last time I visited, Tokyo was ill with the fever and the next day he died. I was very sad. Soon after his death I too became ill with the fever. Memories of my stay in the mission hospital are blurred and within a couple of months I was sent to Happiness Inn. That's a story all of its own.

I vividly remember the last time I spent the night in the oxygen tent. It was in the early hours of the morning, suicide time, Nurse McPherson calls it, when all of a sudden I awoke and like a revelation it hit me like a sledgehammer. I realized then that my days on this earth were going to be short, and each precious day that passes will be making it shorter. It was as if a great empty hole had opened up in my heart. The moment of truth I'd been avoiding for months I now had to face. Any thoughts of a normal life span for me were out of the question.'

Emma's lips began to quiver and she had to inhale deeply to compose herself. 'It's all so sad,' she gulped.

' A while ago I'd fooled myself into believing that my asthma attacks were getting less and less over the months and that the time would come when they would be a thing of the past, but all that was just wishful thinking.

Disappointment overwhelmed me and I had to fight back tears of frustration and rage. I desperately want to live. Being a cripple doesn't bother me anymore. It had become only a minor problem.

The next few days were really terrible. Living with the thought that my life could end with the next asthma attack was terrifying. A lousy, lonely, tight and painful feeling stuck to me like glue. Man, it was scary. I tried to imagine it away but it was impossible. For confirmation I questioned Nurse McPherson, hoping against hope she would tell me I was wrong, but I could sense by her evasive replies and the sad look in her eyes, that she knew it to be so.

Then, out of the blue, I found a small card in a library book. Funny enough the book's title was 'The Power of One' written by someone called Courtenay. Once I'd read the book I found it such an inspiration. One person can make a difference, which means that *everyone of us can contribute something to the world. It made me realize that even though my body's a crock, my mind's a magic castle. Man, this nearly blew my mind and it lifted me out of the dungeon I had crawled into.*

Getting back to the card. On it were a few lines of a poem.

The woods are lovely, dark and deep
But I have promises to keep
And miles to go before I sleep

The words leapt out at me and I knew what I had to do. I would live what time I had left to the full and get as many miles as I could before I too, would sleep.

This gave me a wonderful sense of freedom. I now had an objective, a purpose.

Suddenly I had a flashback to the time when I was in the mission hospital during my illness.

One night my fever soared. When finally I fell asleep I dreamt that gentle strong hands were lifting me up and carrying me to the edge of a forest where a cool breeze fanned across my face. A peace, such as I'd never experienced before came over me and I wanted to stay forever. But I woke up with a nurse shaking and calling, 'Ralph, wake up! Wake up!'

Opening my eyes I saw concern in her eyes.

'You were lying so still I was worried about you,' she explained, feeling my forehead. 'My, your temperature has dropped.'

I'm convinced that someone, call him my ancestral spirit for want of a better name, had come to take me to the other side, but it wasn't yet my time.

A day or so after my new resolution to live life to the full, Dr Stephenson sent me to the laboratory to deliver a specimen. From the first moment of arriving there I was completely captivated by the work. Dr Mostert must have read the look on my face for he suggested I stay. When later he invited me to call as often as I liked, I thought I would burst with the joy I felt. I made up my mind there and then that I wanted to become a medical technologist.

I'm rushing too far ahead. I want to go back to the time Emma arrived at the school.'

Emma gasped and quickly closed the pages. Leaning back on the bed her heart began to thump. Did she really want to know what he had written about her? She felt as if she had been looking deep into Ralph's soul, like a Peeping Tom.

Tense and afraid of what was to come, but at the same time curious, she opened the pages.

'When I first set eyes on Emma I knew there would be something special between us. Funny how sometimes you know right away when you meet someone that they are going to be important to you. But I had a rude awakening when I heard the vicious way she attacked Elizabeth. How dare this upstart and spoilt brat insult someone as caring as Elizabeth! Boy, was I mad! I almost had a frothy on the spot! At least she did have the grace to blush and apologize, but I became wary of her. She was too bitchy and stuck up for my liking. Rich white brat, I thought, we could do without her kind. I decided to avoid her as far as possible.'

Memory of her first day came rushing back and she felt uncomfortable and ashamed. 'I've changed a lot since then,' she whispered.

'It didn't take me long to discover that she was running away from her problems. But she does have the cutest little nose. It always amuses me how, when she is angry or pretends she doesn't care about something, she tilts it heavenwards, like cocking a snoot at the world in general.'

Emma blushed and rubbed her nose. 'Now I know why he always seemed to be laughing at me.'

'I admire her determination and know once she stops running away from herself she'll go far. Her spirit of adventure and humour will help her a lot. She'll also have to learn to accept the things she cannot change. Easy to say but not so easy to do, and who should know that more than me. I've often wanted to tell her that its fine to aim for the moon, but if you can't get there to be satisfied with being one of the stars.

My sympathy went out to her the day I found her lying in a crumpled heap on the floor. She had been trying to walk without crutches. Somehow I'm convinced she'll manage it one day, but not yet.

My biggest shock was when she came to see me in the sick bay during my incarceration, good word that, in the oxygen tent. I fancied her big time and the look on her face told me what I had hoped for, that she liked me as much as I liked her. But she had no future with me because I have no future. This hurt man, did it hurt? My spirits dropped to rock bottom.

The hopelessness of my situation began to wear me down at times and even though it would annoy her I decided to avoid her as much as possible so that when the time comes for me to go she won't get hurt.'

Emma thought back to the time when Ralph had been rude to her for no reason and suddenly all the pieces of the puzzle fell into place.

'I soon abandoned this plan. I missed her too much. Today I'm going to invite her to come with me to the laboratory. I'm sure she'll find it interesting.

The kiss!'

Emma blushed. He had ringed the two words.

'After I had kissed Emma, I felt so embarrassed. What had got into me? I hastened down the corridor and into my room. My heart was pounding like a jungle drum. Putting my hands to my hot face I gasped, 'I'm an imbecile! What's she going to think of me now?' That sudden impulsive action could mean the end of our friendship. I sat brooding for a while and then had to smile. I touched my lips. There had been a small spark, like a minor electric shock, when our lips met. Surely she must have felt it too? Of course, it could have been imagination on my part, or even wishful thinking. But my whole body tingled and I liked the feeling.

'I too felt it, Ralph,' she whispered, touching her lips.

'I know she likes me. There was a soft, gentle look on her face when she touched my arm and she blushed like a tomato. That's the problem with these whiteys, their faces turn such a brilliant red everyone can recognize when they are embarrassed.'

Emma's face burned and she chuckled. 'You're so right, Ralph, so very right.'

'I don't know what got into me. Where do you get off black boy from a rural village in Mpumalanga, and a cripple nogal, to think Emma, who comes from a sophisticated, wealthy white family would want to get together with you? I had to laugh at my stupidity. What

am I going on about? We're not getting married, only trying to have a relationship. Is that a national disaster? We both have some growing up to do, if I live that long, so cool it mate! My problem is how to handle what I've done when I see her again? You just don't go around kissing girls. I'll do it the easy way and pretend it didn't happen.'

The diary ended.

Emma gave a light, breathless laugh and lay back on the pillow deep in thought. An hour or so later, a feeling of exhaustion came over her, and she fell asleep.

****

CHAPTER TWELVE

Get a life.

Emma woke suddenly when she heard the tea bell. The room was filled with sunshine. It covered her like a warm blanket. She felt so much better and lay back on the bed trying to find answers to all sorts of questions. Her mind drifted back to the days when she was still living at home. They were a close-knit family. It all seemed such a long time ago, in another world. Life had been so easy, so comfortable. Each day when she woke up she knew exactly what she wanted and expected. Most of her life had been centered on gymnastics to the exclusion of everything else. She had no real friends, only the people at the gym. She didn't miss not having a friend and felt complete and happy as she was.

Then things went horribly wrong. The shock of her injury and the loss of the use of her legs had shattered her warm, secure world and, at the time, she thought it would be forever.

Her arrival at Happiness Inn had been a revelation. She didn't know why she was so surprised to find the children normal in every way except for their physical disabilities. No, that wasn't quite true, she told herself, the children here seemed to be happier, constantly joking about their handicaps. And their teacher, Mr. Webster, was an inspiration on his own and never once did she hear him lose his temper. Occasionally, like Elizabeth and Ralph, the children too had their 'down' moments like any normal child would have.

With a wave of her hand she muttered, 'No one can constantly live on cloud nine. Mom has told me that on numerous occasions.'

Coming back to the present, she found thoughts of Ralph's passing didn't hurt as much as before. It was as if they had shared another time another planet. For some reason, after reading his diary, a strange kind of freedom and peace had come over her, like she had suddenly found herself. She still had an ache somewhere deep in her heart, which would always be there for she would miss not seeing him or talking to him. Yet she had to move on, but that didn't make the past go away. After all he had been a very good friend.

No, that wasn't quite correct, he was more than a friend. The way Ralph had lived his life was to her a kind of comfort, like a beacon of hope.

A number of pleasant thoughts came to her. The serious way Ralph read the stories for the blind children and his determination to make them come alive in the minds of the listeners. The time he spent training her to read stories. His eagerness to show her around the laboratory and the way he explained, in detail, how the tests were performed. She frowned. Ralph was convinced that one day she would walk without the aid of crutches. She pondered over this for a while and ran her fingers tenderly along the bruise on her elbow and smiled. It would be an uphill battle but maybe, who knows, she could win. Suddenly she realized even that didn't matter to her anymore.

Wrinkling her nose she gave a big sigh. Things had once again changed for her. The here and now is what counts. She would always remember the good times she and Ralph had and be glad they had them. All she needed to do was close her eyes and they'd come to her like a video being played back. She bit her lip before muttering, 'There'll be another change when Elizabeth leaves at the end of the year. Just thinking about it gives me the heebies. But I can't worry about that either,' she reasoned. 'I'll wait until it happens. Mother did hint there was a possibility I may spend the Christmas holidays at home. I didn't take much notice of her at the time because I had Ralph on my mind. Now I would love it to happen, but I mustn't build up my hopes just yet in case it's not to be.'

Noticing the book beside her she picked it up. It was entitled, 'The Principles of Medical Technology'. 'Mmh, interesting,' she murmured. Glancing at her watch she gasped, 'After five! How time has flown. Tea is long over.' She decided to take the book back to the laboratory. 'I hope someone's still there,' she murmured. 'Ralph did tell me that Dr Mostert worked until six each evening.' Climbing down from the bed she placed the book in her jacket pocket and made her way out of the building to the clinic.

A baboon barked somewhere in the veld and a few hadidahs circled overhead and let out their raucous cries. The cool air blew on her face, but she hardly noticed it.

Dr Mostert was alone in the laboratory when she arrived. He seemed pleased to see her. She handed the book to him. 'Nurse McPherson asked me to return this to you,' she explained. 'It was found amongst Ralph's belongings.'

He took the book and placed it on a table nearby.

Looking at her with sad blue eyes he said softly, 'Emma, my dear, we were all shocked to hear about Ralph.' He drew up a chair and helped her to be seated before continuing, 'Ralph certainly enjoyed working in the lab. He would have made a dedicated medical technologist. Who knows, the world may have lost a brilliant scientist.'

She nodded, moistening her dry lips. 'He seemed to know a lot of what was being done here, and he loved the work.' She paused and swallowed uncomfortably. After taking a deep breath, she offered cautiously, 'I too found it very interesting and absorbing and wondered if I could come here whenever I have the chance. I promise not to be a nuisance.'

Dr Mostert smiled. 'Certainly you can. I noticed how you listened so intently as Ralph explained all the bits and pieces we have here. Gradually, like Ralph, you'll learn enough to help with some of the minor tests we do, of which we get plenty.' He pointed to the book. 'Maybe you'd like to have this. It will give you a good introduction into medical technology. I gave it to Ralph, but I should have inscribed his name in it.' He drew a pen from his dust jacket, opened the book and wrote:

To Emma du Preez
From J van A Mostert.

Emma read the inscription and smiled. 'Thank you, Doctor, thank you!' she exclaimed, and carefully placed the book back into her pocket. 'I'll spend as much time as I can studying this so that I'll have some knowledge about what's going on here.'

Dr Mostert rubbed his chin thoughtfully. 'I'd like to suggest that you use your wheelchair when coming here, Emma. I suppose Ralph did explain the reason why.'

'Yes he did. I'll do just that,' Emma put in enthusiastically, 'I'm grateful to you. I must go now. It's almost time for supper. Once again many thanks.'

Dr Mostert helped her to her feet and after handing her the crutches, held the door open for her.

'Bye Doctor.'

'Goodbye, Emma. I look forward to your coming here.'

As she made her way back a feeling of excitement rose up in her at the thought of starting something fresh and new. It came to her that Mother and Father had told her she would find talents she didn't know she had. At the time she had been too angry to believe them. Could it be possible she had found her vocation in life? Time alone would tell.

She brightened as something came as a sudden illumination to her. 'I would also like to carry on reading stories for the blind children. One day I would like to be an actress on the radio and maybe a reader of news on the television or radio.' She grinned. 'As Ralph once said to me, 'My options are improving by the minute.' Life had suddenly taken on a new meaning and her confidence soared.

Just before she entered the grounds of Happiness Inn she stopped and looked towards the west. The hills that Ralph had pointed out to her looked lovely, dark and drenched in mystery making them almost forbidding, but their peaks were bright with a pink and orange glow from the rays of the dying sun.

She stood transfixed. Slowly the brightness faded and the hills became blended into the gathering darkness. Thoughts of her koppie adventure with Elizabeth brought a smile to her lips. Even though it was hair raising at the time, she never once had a nightmare about it. Instead, she and Elizabeth shared many a laugh when they thought back to their ordeal.

When she reached the entrance she heard the sound of laughter from deep within the building and thought again of Ralph. His memory would always be with her, burnt into her mind. She stopped when she saw a single star shining against the evening sky. For a moment she thought she saw Ralph's smiling face among the cloud pictures. A trick of the shadows, of course, she assured herself. Feeling for the book in her pocket she said softly, 'Thank you Ralph, for being what you are, an inspiration to me,' and continued on her way.

That evening, when Emma and Elizabeth were walking to the dining room, they met up with Nurse McPherson who was wheeling a young man towards them. He wore a blue polo-necked sweater and blue jeans. 'Meet our new arrival, Anand Pillay,' she said breezily.

Emma looked at him curiously. She supposed he could be called good-looking. He was about Ralph's age, but with the build of a sportsman. His thick black hair fell straight to his collar and was ruffled as though he regularly ran his fingers through it. His whole bearing was one of antagonism. She wanted to burst out laughing. He reminded her of someone she knew very well.

She smiled to herself. Talk about bad vibes oozing from someone! We have another rebellious Emma du Preez type, she thought, wryly. I'll give him a wide berth until he settles down.

Nurse McPherson explained, 'Anand injured his spine in a horse riding accident some eight weeks ago.

There was a momentary silence.

Elizabeth broke the silence by saying in her usual warm and friendly way, 'Welcome, Anand. I'm sure you'll be happy here.'

'Thanks,' he grunted, barely managing a frosty smile.

Emma looked into his dark smoldering eyes, so large they seemed to swallow his face, but said nothing. He stared back at her with cold indifference. A feeling of irritation swept over her and an angry retort rose to her lips. She had to bite her lip hard to stop it from rushing out.

She wanted to tell him to get a life. Instead, she merely smiled knowingly and went on her way. The end

BEFORE I SLEEP

GLOSSARY

Eina   explanation of pain

Foeitog   shame   - poor thing

Hadidahs   type of bird

Khaya   hut

Koppie   small hill

Mampara   silly

Nogal   what's more

Epilogue

It didn't take long for Emma to discard her crutches. She managed to walk, awkwardly at first, but soon caught up with the other children.

The months seemed to fly past and the time came for her to write her finals, which she passed with ease.

By this time she had spent a few holidays at home and was excited when she was picked up for the last time.

She attended Wits University and obtained a teacher's degree and given a post at her old school. There, she fell in love with the Mathematics master. They married and had twin boys.

When the boys attended school she began to write her memoirs. On completion she sent it to a story competition, winning first prize. She was thrilled to be told that the book was to be published.

****